Chances

by Shardae

ISBN 978-0578-603544

Library of Congress Control Number: 2019916398

Cover image: Shardae Jones

Cover designer: Theresa Linen

Editor: Theresa Linden

Printed in the United States of America

Dedication

I want to dedicate this book to all the young ladies out there that wanted the love of their father. Sometimes a man doesn't know how to properly love his child because he might have grown up without a father himself. We as women must learn to forgive, even if a person isn't deserving of it. Without forgiveness, you'll have many different emotions going on inside your head that you didn't even know you had. So, forgive and live your best life!

Acknowledgments

First off, I want to thank my Lord and Savior, Jesus Christ, for everything He has done for me! Without Him, I am Nothing!

I want to thank my partner in crime, my other whole, my best friend, my king, my husband, Phillip. Thank you for putting up with me. You make it so easy to fall in love with you more and more each day.

I want to thank my son, Elijah, who keeps me going.

Tyria, Quamaine, and Mommy, I love y'all!

I hope you all enjoy reading this! God Bless!

"When it comes to twenty-five-year-old Im'Unique, Ronald, you are the father!" Maury Povich said as he read the DNA test results and stared at the man that sat next to him. The cameraman panned to the studio audience as they went wild, cheering and clapping.

Im'Unique's mother, a well-dressed woman in her early fifties, sat two chairs away from Ronald. She leaned forward, pointed her finger at him and blurted out, "I told you, I told you."

Tears streaked the faces of all three guests that sat on the stage. The audience had now quieted, eager to hear what Ronald had to say.

Still teary-eyed, Ronald stood up brushing the tears from his face with the back of his hands. He buttoned his gray suit jacket and strutted over to Im'Unique.

"I am so happy right now. I'm so sorry I didn't know. I had no idea there was a possibility that you could be my daughter." Ronald spoke standing directly in front of Im'Unique, and she looked him in his eyes, holding his gaze. "I had no idea that your mom was even pregnant back then. When she reached out to me last month and told me that I had a daughter, I-I-I didn't know how to feel."

Ronald took the napkin from his top pocket and wiped the tears from his eyes. "But now, knowing the results, I-I feel like the luckiest man on earth. I promise from this day forward, I will do everything in my power to be a great father to you." Ronald sobbed.

Im'Unique sat frozen for a moment, tears glistening in her big, beautiful honey-brown eyes, while the audience waited with bated breath. Seconds later, she slid off her chair and flung herself into her father's arms. Tears formed rivulets down her cheeks.

I shut the TV off, got up off the couch, and wiped my eyes. I'd never cried watching the *Maury Povich Show* before—I was a grown woman, after all, a twenty-one-year-old housekeeper at the Holiday Inn—but this episode had me full of tears. I wanted to meet my own father.

My heart turned to God as it often did when things seemed impossible or when it ached. *"Lord, first of all, I just wanna say thank you, thank you for my life and allowing me to see another day. Lord, I come asking you to allow me to meet my father. Seeing this show really did something to me, and I want to know what life would be like with a father. I wanna thank you in advance, in Jesus' name. Amen."*

Ride-or-Die Saints

I searched the entire house as I seemed to have misplaced one of my silver four-inch heels that I wanted to wear to church. After searching for an hour, I finally found it in Li'l T's toy box. Almost two years had passed since Li'l T and I moved out of my mother's house. The transmission in my car had gone out, so I had to spend my savings to repair it. I lost my job at the Holiday Inn six months ago, and my bills began to fall behind.

Life got real for me! I began to pray and ask God why it had to be this way, but He reminded me that He would never put more on me than I could bear. I began to seek Him much more than I ever had before. I went to church every time the doors were open. Sometimes we had church service five to six days a week, and I made sure I was there.

Pastor Bernard had gotten installed as the Bishop, so that meant he had more responsibilities, and the more responsibilities for him, the more church for us. But I didn't mind. I loved going to church; it got my mind off my problems. If Bishop Bernard were to go to another church and preach, I would be there, whether it was in town or not. Bishop Bernard always knew that he could count on my mom and me to follow him wherever he went to preach. We were his ride-or-die saints.

Bishop Bernard was a middle-aged, dark-skinned, slim-built preacher that always wore the sharpest dress suits—just like the famous Steve Harvey. I loved the way he preached; he could tear up the whole church. I've known Bishop for over a decade. If I ever needed him, he was there for my family and me. When I went through the roughest time in my life with all the complications with Li'l T, Bishop Bernard was there, praying me through, and I would always be grateful to him for that.

I arrived thirty minutes late for church, but I didn't miss a beat because they were still singing praise and worship. I sat in my usual seat on the left side of the church. The sunlight peeked through the window, hitting my body and making me warm and comfortable. The choir sang and lifted my spirits high. Time seemed to fly by as we sang, praised, and listened as Bishop Bernard preached.

Then he said something that made time stand still. Bishop Bernard was preaching, and he spoke about how a miracle was going to take place in the next twenty-four hours. Everyone danced and rejoiced in the Lord over what was to come.

After church, my mom and I stopped at the gas station. I stayed in the car while she went in. As she returned to the car, a man was walking beside her. Several of his features resembled mine: he was light skinned with a wide nose, and he had nice full round lips just like mine. Judging the man's height as he walked next to my mom, he didn't look much taller than me. He was bald with no wrinkles, and he looked to be in his early forties. I loved the color of his skin; it looked like he'd wiped True Match beige foundation all over his body.

The stranger came to my side of the car, smiling uncontrollably as my mom stood next to him. I couldn't help but smile back at him. If a person didn't know us, I'm sure they'd think we'd known each other for years, the way we were smiling at one another. I couldn't explain it, but I felt a connection with him.

"Hi, young lady," the unknown man said as he bent over to talk through my half-open window.

"Hi," I replied.

"Do you know who I am?"

"No." *How am I supposed to know who you are?*

"I'm Andy."

"Moore?" The last name came to mind the moment he said Andy.

"Yes." His smile grew even bigger as I guessed his last name correctly.

My heart raced as if I had just run two miles. I'd waited for this moment, and now that I was twenty-one years old, it was finally here. I'd waited for the day that I could call someone DAD. I couldn't believe this was happening now.

"Wow!" was all I could say. All I wanted was for him to take me into his arms and hug me as if I were his little girl that had been lost, and finally found. "So, how are you?" I said not knowing what else I should say.

"I'm doing good," he said with a smile. "I'm even better now that I've met you. You are so beautiful. It's funny because I have a picture of me when I was younger, and you look just like me."

"Really?" I asked.

"Yeah, I'm gonna look for it, and hopefully one day I can show you, if that's OK with you."

"Yeah, that'll be fine." I smiled back.

"So, can I have a hug?" Andy asked as his smile weakened, as if he was scared I might say no.

"Sure." I stepped out of the car and gave him a hug.

"Ahh, it's so nice to meet you, young lady," Andy said as we broke away. "I think we can make this work." He looked me in the eyes as he spoke.

"Make what work?" I asked confused.

"Us, and building a relationship with each other. If that's OK with you?" Andy asked again with a weak smile.

"Yeah, for sure," I said with excitement. "I didn't have you growing up, but we could work it out. Maybe you and my son will have a better relationship."

"You have a son?" Andy's face lit up and his eyes grew bigger.

"Yes, I have a four-year-old. Li'l T, come say hi to your granddad." I opened the back door, unbuckled Li'l T's seat belt and picked him up to introduce him to Andy.

"What's up, little man?" Andy asked Li'l T, holding out his hand for a handshake.

Instead of taking his hand, Li'l T decided to make a joke, as he often did. "This is yo grandaddyyyyyy!" Li'l T sang as if he was Mr. Brown off Medea.

We all laughed in unison. At four years old, Li'l T was always doing or saying something to make everyone laugh.

"Li'l man is a comedian, I see." Andy laughed.

"Yeah, he is." I nodded my head.

"Well, what's your number?" Andy asked, changing the subject. "Can I call you sometime?" He seemed hesitant, probably unsure about my answer.

"Sure." I smiled at him. "I'd like that a lot." I reached into the car and grabbed my cell phone out of the cup holder.

Andy dialed my number right after I gave it to him so that I could have his number, too. I was overcome with joy because I finally met Andy. *Was this the miracle that Bishop Bernard was talking about?*

After I buckled Li'l T into his booster seat, I pulled out my cell phone to call my mom and tell her that I was on the way to her house. I hit the "contacts" button and the first name that came up was Andy's. It had been two weeks and I hadn't heard from him since we exchanged numbers. I'd been so excited to finally meet him. I didn't want to call him; I figured if he wanted to talk, then he would call me first.

"Andy hasn't even called yet," I stated to my mom as I sat at her house like I often did. "Was he serious when he said that we could make this work, or was he just lying?" My feelings were hurt.

"Maybe he's been busy," my mom replied, looking over at me from her recliner chair, "or maybe he wants to call you, but he just doesn't know what to say."

"He could find *something* to say. He could try to get to know me, find out what I like, what I dislike. Or maybe explain where he's been all these years," I ranted.

"I'm sure he'll call, Keisha," my mom calmly said.

"Who cares if he does or if he doesn't? I've made it this long without talking to him, so it's not like it will make me or break me." I folded my arms across my chest.

I was lying on my mom's couch watching the movie *What's Eating Gilbert Grape,* staring Leonardo DiCaprio and Johnny Depp, when my phone rang. Andy's number popped up on the screen, and I instantly felt butterflies—happy but also mad that it had taken him so long to call me.

"Hello," I answered.

"Hey, young lady, how are you?" Andy asked.

"I'm good, and you?"

"I'm doing good. I've been meaning to call you, but I've been really busy lately. You were on my mind, so I decided to call you."

"It' OK. You called me now and that's what matters."

"So, what are you up to?"

"I'm at my mom's house, waiting until it's time to go to church," I replied.

"Yeah, I know. She called me asking why I haven't called you yet," Andy said.

I pursed my lips. *So, I wasn't just on his mind like he claimed I was.* "So, if my mom didn't call you, would you have called me?" I questioned him.

"Well, no, I mean yeah I-I would have called you eventually . . . Listen this is new to me, but I'm going to try to do my best to make it work."

"It's new to me, too," I blurted out with attitude. "Well, how about this: let's just forget about the past and move forward. You weren't a part of my life growing up, but maybe you can be a part of my future and your grandson's future."

"Yeah, I'd like that a lot. So . . . where do we begin? Uh, how old are you?"

"Twenty-one."

"Well, that makes you my oldest child."

"Oh, wow, how many kids do you have?" I was eager to know how many other siblings I had.

"Including you, I have six."

"Are you a part of all of their lives?"

"Well, yeah the ones that want me to be a part of their lives. Anyway, tell me a bit about yourself. What do you like doing?" Andy quickly changed the subject.

"I love to eat!" I laughed, but it was true. "I enjoy going to church, I enjoy reading, and I like to go line dancing."

"That's cool. I love to eat too. Can you cook? I work at a restaurant and I'm the cook. Maybe one day we can go to the park and I could put some steaks on the grill. I'm a pretty good cook," Andy bragged.

"Yeah, that sounds fun. We could all get to know each other a little better."

"Right. So you go to church a lot, I see."

"Yeah, I do. Do you go to church?" I asked.

"I haven't been to church in so long. I don't remember the last time that I went."

"Well, maybe one day you could go with me."

"Yeah, maybe one day. Hey, well, I just called to check up on you." He changed the subject again. "How about I give you a call later on?"

"OK, that's fine," I replied.

"OK, talk to you later, young lady."

After Andy and I got off the phone, I got ready to go to church. Church was great. Bishop Bernard preached on getting into your rightful position. That could mean getting into the correct position with God, getting in position with the church and doing different things to help make yourself an active member, or simply getting in position with a career move. It could mean many things, but I knew that I had to get in my position and do more for myself and make myself better.

~ ~ ~

It was nine thirty at night and I had just tucked Li'l T into bed when my phone rang. Andy's number popped up. *I forgot he said he'd call me back.*

"Hello," I answered.

"Hey, young lady, I just called to say good night and to see if I could take you and the baby out for ice cream next Wednesday?"

"Aw, thank you. Good night to you too, and yes of course you can." I smiled.

"OK, I'll try to call you soon, or you could call me."

"OK." I hung up the phone still smiling. I could get used to speaking with Andy as long as he's willing to try to get to know me.

~ ~ ~

I met Andy at the ice cream parlor on Wednesday. There we talked and I found out that he enjoyed fishing and golfing. He asked if he could take Li'l T and me fishing one day, and of course I had no problem with it. Andy played ball with Li'l T while I enjoyed watching. We spent all day together and it was amazing. I loved being around my dad; it was such a good vibe and there was nothing but fun and laughter the entire time.

The sun had vanished into the clouds and the sky had gotten darker. It was getting late, so we decided that we should head back to the house so that I could put Li'l T to bed.

"I had a great time today, Andy. I could tell Li'l T did too," I said as we slowly sashayed to the car.

"Yeah, I did, too, young lady. It was nice for a first time." Andy stopped to look me in the eyes. "We definitely have to do it again soon," he said with a smile.

"Yes, for sure, I would like that a lot." I smiled back. "Would you like to come to church with me on Sunday?" I asked, hoping he would agree to come.

"You know what, young lady, I think I might just take you up on your offer." His smile never left.

"OK, great! I will see you on Sunday then."

We said our goodbyes.

~ ~ ~

I was getting dressed for church when my phone rang.

"Hello," I answered on speaker phone as I was applying mascara to my eye lashes.

"Good morning, young lady. How are you today?" Andy replied on the other end.

"I'm blessed by the best. How are you?"

"I'm wonderful. I was calling because I didn't know if you wanted me to drive myself to church or if you wanted me to pick y'all up?"

"You could pick us up if you'd like." I smiled at the idea of my father and me going to church together.

"OK cool, I was hoping you'd say that, because I didn't want to go in by myself and have everyone staring at me."

I laughed. "The saints wouldn't stare at you. They would just hug on you. We are a church that hugs everyone."

"Oh, wow." He laughed, too. "Well, I am on my way. Be there in about fifteen minutes."

"OK, Li'l T and I are ready." I hung up the phone and applied some blush on my cheeks and gloss on my lips.

~ ~ ~

Church was amazing. Bishop Bernard preached the message "You can't change the past, but you can change the future." I knew that applied to Andy as well as myself. He was unknown in my past, but I could certainly know him now and in the future. After church Andy took Li'l T and me out to eat.

"So, how did you enjoy the service at church?" I asked Andy as we sat down across from each other at the steak house restaurant.

"I really enjoyed myself. I felt like the preacher was talking to me the entire time."

"Yeah, that's how it goes when God is getting your attention."

"Hey listen." Andy grabbed my hand and pulled it a bit closer to himself. "I'm sorry about the past. I know I can't change it. But I promise you, young lady, that I will try to do better in the future. I will be a better grandfather than I was a father." Andy teared up.

"It's OK. We can let the past be the past and move forward in our relationship." My eyes also became teary.

"Hi, my name is Natalie"—the waitress came over, interrupting our heartfelt moment—"and I will be your server this afternoon. Can I start you all off with something to drink?"

Both Andy and I wiped our eyes with the napkins on the table and then ordered our food and drinks. After we ate, we went back to my place. Andy spent the entire day with Li'l T and me again. We watched the basketball game as the Cleveland Cavaliers beat the Golden State Warriors. We were very happy and excited to see Cleveland, Ohio, winning the championship.

After we cheered on the Cavs, Li'l T insisted on watching *Peppa Pig* on Nick Jr. We sat without speaking, listening to the silly show, Li'l T's occasional giggles, and the sound of crickets coming through the open living room window. Once the show ended, Andy helped put Li'l T to bed.

"OK, young lady, once again I enjoyed myself." Andy smiled at me as he walked towards the front door and fidgeted with his car keys.

"I enjoyed myself too, Andy." I smiled back at him and followed him to the door. "What time do you have to go into work tomorrow?"

"I'm working second shift tomorrow." He stopped and turned around so that we would be face-to-face.

"Well, if you want to come over in the morning, I'll make breakfast for us."

"How about I come over and *I* make breakfast in the morning?" he said, pointing to himself. "I'll bring everything that I need."

"OK then." I shrugged my shoulders.

"You won't have to do anything but wash the dishes when I'm done." He chuckled.

I laughed with him. "Deal." I extended my right hand. "See you in the morning."

"Alright then." Andy shook my hand.

"Well, you have a good night."

"You too, beautiful," Andy said as he walked out the door.

If this is what having a dad feels like, I wish I would've had one a long time ago. Having Andy around has brought more joy and excitement into my life. I love it when he's around Li'l T and me. I love getting to know him and I love doing things with him. In the past, it was always my mother doing things with me, but now I get to experience life with Andy.

~ ~ ~

The next morning, I woke up to Li'l T kissing me on my cheek.

"Mommy, wake up, wake up, Mommy," Li'l T said as he patted me on my shoulder.

"I'm awake, baby. Good morning." I gave him a smile and kissed his forehead.

My cell rang, interrupting our sweet moment. It was Andy saying that he would be over in thirty minutes. Li'l T and I brushed our teeth and went downstairs to wait for Andy to come. Li'l T saw Andy's car and opened the door for him.

"Hi, Andy," Li'l T said, jumping up and down with excitement.

"Hey, li'l man, how are you doing today?" Andy leaned down to kiss him on the cheek.

"Is that for me?" Li'l T's eyes grew wider when he saw the bags in Andy's hands.

"Yes, it's for you and your mom." Andy walked into the kitchen and set the bags on the table.

"Hello, young lady, how are you today?" Andy asked me.

"I'm blessed by the best. Do you need any help?" I followed him into the kitchen.

"No, ma'am." He started taking the groceries out of the bag. "OK, young lady, no disrespect, but I want you to get out of the kitchen and don't come in until I say so." Andy playfully shoved me out of the kitchen.

"Um, OK, I guess," I replied, confused, but I did as I was told. "I will be upstairs giving Li'l T a bath. Holler if you need anything."

"Just go and handle yo' business, young lady. I got this," Andy said in a cocky way.

An hour went by before Andy called us down for breakfast. I entered the kitchen and couldn't believe my eyes. An entire buffet of food lined my kitchen table, as well as the countertop. He'd made many different options to choose from. The table was filled with bacon, turkey bacon, sausage, turkey sausage, ham, and there were scrambled eggs, some with cheese and some without cheese. He'd made biscuits, toast, pancakes, and French toast, even fried potatoes. On the countertop, sat a fruit platter filled with strawberries, melons, pineapples, grapes, cantaloupe, and whole fruit with apples, and oranges. He also had different flavors of yogurt parfaits.

"Wow, Andy, I wasn't expecting all this," I said with my hand over my mouth. "If I had cooked, it was going to be something simple like bacon, toast, and eggs." I laughed.

He laughed too. "I would've eaten it. I'm sorry, I didn't know what you like. Guess I should have asked first, but I wanted y'all to have options to choose from." He sounded sincere.

"Yes, you definitely gave us options," I replied, still amazed. "So, who's going to eat all this?"

"Us, and what is left over, you can eat later."

"OK, well let's eat." I got three plates from the kitchen cupboard.

We ate in silence as we filled our bellies with Andy's delicious breakfast. After breakfast, Andy helped clean the kitchen and put the food away. It was soon time for him to leave for work, so I packed him some lunch and he was on his way. Then I called my mom so that she and my siblings could come over and have breakfast.

The Love of a Father

I sat in my room, gazing out the window and letting the sun warm my face. For the past two months, Andy and I had been talking every day and hanging out more. We planned to go to the Fair this afternoon, and I couldn't wait.

My cell phone rang, and I answered on the third ring, still looking out the window.

"Hey, Keisha, it's me, you know, YOUR MOM. You haven't been over in a few weeks, what's up?"

"Um, I know who it is, MOTHER. I've been hanging with Andy and today we're going to the County Fair."

"Oh, really." My mom sounded disappointed or a little sad.

"Yes."

"Well, bring Li'l T over. He could stay with me while the two of you go."

"No, Mom, I want him to come with us," I rudely said. "We'll come over when we leave the Fair if it's not too late." I tried to soften my tone.

"What do you mean, if it's not too late? Keisha, you know you and Li'l T can come over whenever y'all want to. It don't matter what time!" my mom yelled over the phone. "You're starting to act funny since you've been hanging around Andy. I'm happy you're getting to know him, Keisha, I really am, but that doesn't mean just shut your mother out."

"I'm not shutting you out, Mother. I'm sorry you feel that way."

"I just don't want him to hurt you. You're my baby girl, and he can't just enter your life and act like he's the world's greatest dad."

"I know, Mom." A car horn beeped just outside. "Well, he's here now, so I gotta go. I'll call you when we get back. I love you." I hung up the phone.

True, I'd been spending a lot of time with Andy, but my mom needed to accept the fact that he was in my life now and he wasn't going anywhere.

"Hey, Andy." I buckled Li'l T into the back seat.

"Hey, young lady, how are you?"

"I'm good." I got into the front seat.

"Hey, li'l man, how are you? Are you ready for the Fair?" Andy asked Li'l T.

"Yes. I not been before." Li'l T bounced in his booster seat.

"You haven't? Well, Paw-Paw is going to take you for your first time, and I'm gonna make sure you enjoy yourself." Andy smiled at Li'l T.

We arrived at the Fair and it was packed. We stood in line for thirty minutes before we entered. The look on Li'l T's face was priceless when we passed through the gates; he was so happy.

"Ohhh, Mommy, Mommy, I want that!" Li'l T pointed to a huge stuffed animal.

"OK, let's go get it." Andy led the way to the stuffed animal.

In order to win the stuffed animal, you had to pay five dollars to throw one ball into a little hole. Andy tried four times before he finally got the ball into the hole and won the stuffed animal. He let Li'l T pick out the one he wanted, which was a big, fuzzy blue bear. Afterwards, we rode rides that Li'l T was able to get on. We walked around and anything Li'l T or I wanted, Andy was sure to get it for us.

We were having such a wonderful time together that I wished I would have had memories like this growing up. I didn't want to think about the past and what I didn't have, so I continued to enjoy myself as if I was a kid. As time went on, I got tired and it was almost Li'l T's bedtime. It was nine thirty at night, and we all were worn out, so we headed back home.

"I had so much fun today, young lady. I'm glad we went," Andy said as we walked to the car.

"Yeah, me too," I replied with a smile. "You didn't have to buy all that stuff for Li'l T though."

"It's OK. That's my li'l man." He smiled. His hands were full of stuffed animals, toys, and a basketball.

I didn't reply. I kept walking as I was overcome with joy because we had such a wonderful time today.

~ ~ ~

I was straightening up my house when I noticed a scarf hanging across the chair. It wasn't just any ol' scarf; My mom had given it to me. It reminded me that I'd been spending a lot of time with Andy and neglecting my mom. I used to visit her every day and just hang out at her house, but Andy had wanted to go out and do different things each day. I haven't had time to visit my mom because we've stayed out all day. I loved my mom with all my heart; she was my best friend, but I'd never had a chance to experience having a father in my life. In a way, I blamed her for keeping him away from me.

I hated that I felt that way, but I couldn't help it. Spending time with Andy made me feel like I'd hit the jackpot. It felt like nothing could ever go wrong when we're together. True, he hadn't been there for me growing up, but he was trying now, and he was being a great grandfather to Li'l T. And we could now catch up on lost time.

"Mommy, I wanna see grandma. I miss grandma." Li'l T bounced into the room, interrupting my thoughts.

In a way, I missed her too, but I still blamed her for not allowing me to meet Andy sooner. She should've done everything she could to make it happen so that I could've had a father in my life.

"OK, baby, I'll take you to see her." I pulled Li'l T into a hug. I couldn't allow myself to keep blaming my mother for something that probably wasn't her fault. I was a mother, so I knew how some men were. Some men walked away from their responsibility, and some just didn't care that they even had a child. I knew this because T acted as if Li'l T just didn't exist.

My phone rang, interrupting my thoughts.

"Hello?" I answered.

"Hey, young lady, how are you today?" Andy asked.

"I'm good. How are you?"

"I'm wonderful. I was hoping to come see you and my grandson today."

"Of course you can, but Li'l T and I were on our way to my mom's house. We haven't seen her in a while and Li'l T misses her."

"What's a while? A week?" Andy said sarcastically.

"Actually, yes! I haven't seen her since Sunday, and that was during church." Andy knew that mom and I were very close.

"You can't let me come take you and Li'l T out for a bit and then go to your mom's house?" Andy insisted.

"No, we're going over there now. We're almost ready, plus my mom is making us dinner."

"OK, well, call me later." Andy sounded sad.

"OK, I will." I hung up and finished getting ready to head to my mom's house.

~ ~ ~

Later that night after I tucked Li'l T into bed, I called Andy, but he didn't answer. I figured he was sleeping because he had to get up for work in the morning. The next day, Andy called me after work.

"Hey, young lady, how are you and my grandson doing today?" he asked.

"We're good. How are you?"

"I'm OK, but I'd be even better if I could come over and take you and my grandson to the movies this evening."

"Aw, I wish you would have told me earlier. My mom already purchased tickets to *The Lion King.*"

"I was hoping WE could go together."

"I'm sorry, but my mom already got them. We are going with her," I blurted out. "Maybe you could come over tomorrow and hang out with us."

Andy made no reply at first and then he shouted into the phone, "We will see." After a pause, he added, "Well, have fun with your MOM. Talk to you later." And he hung up without giving me a chance to reply.

~ ~ ~

Later that night as I was driving home from my mom's house, I called Andy but, again, he didn't answer. He didn't have work in the morning, so I didn't understand why he didn't answer. I waited for him to call me back, but he never did. *He can't possibly be jealous of me hanging with my mom, can he?*

~ ~ ~

The following day Andy texted me, asking if I wanted to hang out. I thought it was weird that he texted because he always called me. So I dialed his number.

"Hey, Andy. How are you today?" I asked.

"I'm doing good. How about you? Did you all enjoy the movie?" His tone of voice was calmer than the last time we spoke.

"Yes, we did." Li'l T had so much fun. He sat on a booster seat munching on popcorn, his eyes riveted to the screen. He didn't get to go to movies often, so it had been a treat.

"Great." Andy sounded disinterested.

"Can I ask you something?"

"Of course you can. What's up?"

"Why did you text instead of calling me?" I sat on the edge of my bed.

"Well, I didn't know if you were with your mother or not. You might not have had time for me today."

"Oh, stop!" I said, laughing. "Anyways, it's hot outside, so I'm going to take Li'l T to Splash Pad. Would you like to join us?"

"Sure, I'll get dressed and be on my way."

"OK, see ya then." I packed a bag for myself and Li'l T.

We went to the local Splash Pad and had lots of fun. Andy taught Li'l T how to swim in the three hours that we were there. Afterwards, we went to a Jamaican restaurant that I had never been to in the next city over. The food was amazing. I never thought I'd try it, but I guess there's a first time for everything.

"Would you like to come in?" I asked Andy as we pulled into my driveway. "I have a fire stick. We could pop some popcorn and find a good movie to watch."

"Yes, young lady, I'd like that." Andy replied with a smile.

Li'l T had fallen asleep during the car ride, so Andy carried him into the house. Of course after laying him on the couch, he woke up. I popped popcorn and searched for a movie to watch. After about ten minutes of searching, Andy and I both agreed on the movie *Unstoppable* starring Denzel Washington.

"Have you ever seen this movie?" Andy asked.

"I think I have, but only pieces of it. I'm sure it's good because Denzel plays in it, and all of his movies are good."

"Yeah, he is pretty dope."

"Yeah, he's amazing! One of my favorite actors. Him and Samuel L. Jackson, I think it's a tie between them two." I nodded my head.

"Really? That's good to know. You learn something new every day." Andy told me Samuel Jackson was also his favorite actor.

After one hour and thirty-eight minutes, the movie ended. Of course I cried at the end; I often got emotional watching movies like this.

"Are you crying?" Andy asked.

"No, I just have something in my eyes," I lied.

"Yeah right. You're crying." Andy stood up and walked over to the couch I was sitting on. "Aw, come here, baby. Daddy's got you." He pulled me up and hugged me tight.

He had never hugged me like this before, and at that moment I realized this was all I'd ever wanted and all I ever needed.

Andy kissed my forehead and looked me in the eye. "I'm happy I got a chance to meet you, young lady," he said with his arms still wrapped around me.

"Me too." I laid my head on his chest because I didn't want him to see that tears forming in my eyes all over again.

"Well, I'd better get going. I have to work in the morning. I'll call you tomorrow. Maybe we can go out to eat or something." Andy broke away and reached for his car keys.

"Well, my mom said she was going to cook a big meal tomorrow and she told me to come over."

"Oh, I see how it is. Your mom, huh? Well, OK, young lady, I will see you later. Have fun with your mom." Andy swung the front door open and stepped outside.

What was the issue with him and my mom? He seemed a little cold every time I mentioned her.

~ ~ ~

The next day I woke up to a text message from an unknown number. "I see some skeletons have come out of the closet. You are 'claiming' to be Andy's daughter. Well, we will see about that."

After reading that text I was fully awake.

"Who is this?" I texted back.

"This is Andy's WOMAN!!!" she replied.

I laughed to myself. If I had a boyfriend and he told me that he met his oldest daughter—one he's never mentioned before—a few months ago, and they've been spending time together, I might not buy that story myself. Instead of replying to the text, I called the number so that I could talk with her, not that I had to explain myself to a random woman but just because I didn't want to text her.

"Hello," she answered with a nasty attitude.

"Hi, I'm Kei—" I was rudely interrupted by her before I could get my full name out.

"I don't care who you are! I found your number in MY man's phone and he's claiming that you are his daughter. I don't believe it! And IF you are his daughter, yo' mama should've been woman enough to tell him YEARS ago instead of waiting until now!"

My blood was boiling. I was OK with her thinking that I was another woman that Andy was seeing. I found that quite comical. *But no one talks about my mama, telling me what she should have done in the past.* Now it was war.

"First of all, don't you ever in your life say anything about my mom. You don't know me, and you don't know her, so you should have kept that comment to yourself, lady," I said with rage.

"Whatever, you young little bitch. I will kick yo' ass and yo' mama's ass too!"

The right thing for me to do at this moment would have been to just hang up the phone, collect my thoughts, and pray, but praying was the last thing on my mind when she called me outta my name.

Hostile words flew out of my mouth. I was calling her names and challenging her. Next thing I knew, I was giving her my address and telling her that I was here now, and I'd be waiting for her.

"You are fucking crazy!" said the woman on the other end of the phone. Without giving me a chance to respond, she hung up on me.

Furious, I called my mom and told her what just happened. Now she was a bit upset too. She wanted me to give her the woman's number, but I didn't because it would have made things worse. After talking with my mom for twenty minutes about

Andy's girlfriend, my nerves calmed down a bit, and I could tell my mom's had calmed too.

"I think I need to pray; I was swearing like a sailor to that broad," I calmly said to my mom, wishing I had never cursed the way I did.

"Yes, me too. I didn't swear out loud, but I had a few choice words in my head that I was thinking." She laughed.

My mom and I prayed and repented before we hung up the phone. I decided to give Andy a call to tell him what had transpired, but he didn't answer the phone. I texted him, but there was no response.

A Fathers Love . . . or Not

Li'l T and I had just gotten home from church. Lately, around this time, I would be expecting a phone call from Andy asking if he could take Li'l T and me out to eat. A week had passed since the incident with Andy's girlfriend, and I hadn't heard anything from him. I'd been calling him every day, but he hadn't answered any of my calls or replied to my text messages. *What did I do wrong? Maybe I shouldn't have cursed at his girlfriend. Maybe I should've just let her speak her piece and let it go.*

Or maybe I should've just ignored the text message. Or maybe I should have let him take Li'l T and I to the movies instead of going with my mom. I questioned myself. *We didn't even get a chance to go to the park and grill steaks yet. Will I ever get to talk to him again?* Tears rolled down my face. Andy wasn't speaking to me, and I felt like it was all my fault.

Two weeks had passed since the incident with his girlfriend

. . .

Still no answer to my phone calls, no reply to my texts. I should have given up and stopped trying, but something in me just wasn't ready to give up yet. Those moments we'd spent together made me realize that all I'd ever wanted was a father in my life. And since I'd now experienced it, I just couldn't give it up that easily. It took twenty-one years to realize that all I wanted was to be loved by a man, but not just any man. I'm talking about the man that should have been the first one to love me. Andy should have been the man to teach me how a woman should be treated. He should have been there for me when I needed him.

All I could do now was think of how I could reconcile with Andy. If he were to call and tell me to get ready, that he was coming to get me, I would be ready to go, looking out the window as if I was a five-year-old little girl waiting for her daddy to pick her up and take her to the candy store. I just didn't understand what I'd done that was so wrong for him to stop talking to me and at least hear my side of the story.

Nineteen days, exactly, since I'd heard from Andy . . .

I decided to text him this one last time to see if he would text me back.

Hey, what's up, Andy? Haven't heard from you in a few days—nineteen days to be exact, but who's counting? LOL. What's a good time for us to get together and hang out? We didn't get a chance to grill the steaks yet. I waited and waited but got no response.

I didn't realize that not having a father in my life could affect me so much, until he actually came into my life and left. I was sick to my stomach thinking about how he was avoiding me. *Maybe he's been in an accident and he's not avoiding me. He just can't get to the phone? Or maybe he's in jail?* I called the local hospital to see if he'd been admitted, but he hadn't. I looked online to see if he had gone to the county jail, but there was no sign of him there either.

~ ~ ~

Six months later, I decided to forget that I had ever met Andy. I hadn't spoken to him since before the conversation with his girlfriend. Bishop Bernard had to preach at another church, and of course his ride-or-die crew went. While there, I noticed a woman that looked a lot like Andy's mom. I knew this because I had met her when I was a young child, and plus my mom told me exactly who she was.

The woman had smooth brown skin; big, lovely, light brown eyes; a nice figure; and no wrinkles, even though she was older.

Maybe what they said was true: *black don't crack*. This woman was absolutely gorgeous. Her hair was nicely done in a shoulder-length curly bob, and I could tell she dressed to impress, because she was fly. She wore a long purple skirt-suit with silver accessories and silver two-inch heels.

I guess the woman sensed me staring at her because she looked in my direction. We stared at each other for a moment, her on one side of the church, and I on the other.

When church ended, I gathered Li'l T's small toys that I had brought to keep him occupied during the service. One of the toy trucks fell underneath the pew, so I kneeled to pick it up. I was on my knees on the floor when I noticed those silver two-inch heels right in front of me. I stood up and got my balance.

The woman and I looked at each other eyeball-to-eyeball as my heart beat a thousand times faster than normal. Without saying anything, she opened her arms and waited for me to come and embrace her.

At that moment, I came to a standstill. I couldn't move, but the woman seemed so harmless. I fell into her arms, and she hugged me as if I'd been her missing child.

"How are you doing, Keisha?" She knew exactly who I was. "You are so beautiful." She looked into my eyes, her smile showing off her beautiful, perfect teeth.

"I'm good, thank you." I smiled back at her.

"I knew exactly who you were when you walked in. I'm your grandma, Ms. Maryanne. Andy told me that you all have been spending time together. I was wondering why you haven't been to my house by now."

"I haven't heard from him in a while now. I think it's been about six months since Andy and I last talked."

"Well, you're gonna have to give me your phone number so I can call you sometimes. Is that OK with you?"

"Yes, ma'am, that's fine."

Ms. Maryanne grabbed a pen from her purse and opened her bible so she could write my phone number down in it. I gave her my number and introduced her to Li'l T. She complimented us and told me how much I looked just like Andy. Of course, I didn't want to hear any of that because Andy was dead to me again. Ms. Maryanne said she would give me a call. I couldn't help but wonder if she was going to be like her son: asking for my number but never using it.

~ ~ ~

The next day as I was driving to the store, an unknown number called me, and I figured it was Andy's mom.

"Hello?" I answered as I pulled into the parking space closest to the entrance.

"Hey, Keisha, this is your grandmother Maryanne. How are you doing today?" she said on the other end of the phone.

"I'm doing well. How are you?" I turned off the ignition to my car.

"I'm OK. I'm going to be over at my daughter's house this evening, and I was wondering if you would like to come over. I told her all about you, and she would like to meet you."

"Um, OK, sure I will come over." I hesitated. "Where does she live?"

"She stays on Maine Avenue, on the east side."

"Oh, wow, I live right around the corner from there," I said, taken by surprise. "I live on Crehore Street."

"Do you really?" Ms. Maryanne sounded surprised too.

"Yep."

"She's been living there for five years now." There was a pause. "It's a shame that we've lived in the same small town and didn't even know how close we were to each other."

"Right. Well, call me when you get there, and Li'l T and I will come over."

"OK, dear, I will see you soon." Ms. Maryanne hung up the phone.

After leaving the store, I went to my mom's house to see what she and the kids were up to.

"So, guess who called me today and wants to see me?" I said to my mom as I walked into her house using the key that I had.

"Andy's mom?" she guessed, always seeming aware of what was going on.

"Yes. I didn't think she would call me so soon. I thought she was going to be like Andy. Do you know I still haven't heard from him?"

"Well, it might be good for you to go over there and get to know them. Despite what Andy did, they are still your family, and if they want a chance to get to know you, then I think it would be good for you to go." My mom sounded sincere.

"Yeah." I shrugged my shoulders. "I guess you're right." I looked in her fridge and grabbed a bottle of water for myself.

While sitting at my mom's, Ms. Maryanne called and told me that she had reached her daughter's house and that I could come over whenever I was ready. I stayed at my mom's an hour longer before I was on my way to see Andy's mom and sister. I was nervous about the visit. Even though they were my blood relatives, they were still strangers to me. I decided I wouldn't stay long; I'd just show my face and leave. Fifteen minutes later, I was knocking at the front door.

"Come in," said a woman on the other side of the door.

I entered the house and Ms. Maryanne and her daughter were walking towards me to greet me with open arms.

"Oh, my God, you look just like Andy, Keisha." The woman appeared to be flabbergasted. "I'm your Aunt Gina," she said while embracing me. Gina was just as beautiful as Ms. Maryanne. She was thin, stood about five-foot-four, and had the most alluring cocoa-black skin and eyes. Her nose was wide, like Andy's, and she had a dimple in both of her cheeks that stood out when she smiled. Even though she had a gap between her two front teeth, she was still beautiful.

"Yeah, I get that a lot," I replied as I broke away from her.

"So, how are you doing?" Gina asked, smiling. "It's good to meet you. Is this your son?"

"Yes, this is Li'l T." I picked up Li'l T and introduced him.

"He's adorable. He looks just like you and Andy."

I wanted Gina to stop talking about how much we looked like Andy because I was trying to block him from my mind. Her bringing him up didn't make it any better.

"Hey, Keisha, you look so beautiful," Ms. Maryanne said.

"Hey, Ms. Maryanne, you think I'm beautiful? Girl, look at you. You killing the game." I stepped back to get a good look at her. "You styling and profiling. I want to dress like you when I get older." I gave her a hug.

"Oh, girl, please. This ain't nothing but something that I threw on." Ms. Maryanne winked at me.

"Have you heard from your dad?" asked Gina.

I shook my head. "Well, I just met him less than a year ago, and things were going good at first. He'd call to check up on me, and we were hanging out doing different things. Then all of a sudden, he stopped calling me. And now, when I call him, he ignores me. I've tried many times to reach out to him, but it seems like he doesn't want to be bothered with me, so I gave up and just stopped calling him."

"That man crazy. You look just like him," Gina shouted.

"People have told me that since I can remember. If I had a dollar for every time someone has told me that, I'd be rich right now," I said with a giggle.

"I'm so sorry about that, Keisha; I don't know what's wrong with that boy." Ms. Maryanne gave me a sympathetic look.

"It's not your fault. It's him. He told me that he and I would go to the park and grill steaks, and that day never came. He went to church with me and we were hanging out pretty much every day for two months, but now he won't even return my calls. I've left him messages and everything, but I've gotten no response.

"Well, I wonder why?" Gina asked.

"Some woman called my phone, trying to argue with me because she found my number in his phone. After that I heard nothing else from him."

"Yeah, that white woman ain't doing nothing but tryna control his life. She hates when he comes over for family functions. She got that man whipped," Gina told us.

"Well, it's not like I'm just some other girl. I'm his daughter, and he shouldn't allow any woman to come between our relationship! He just met me. He should be trying to get to know me the best way he can," I ranted.

"Yeah, I understand, Keisha, and I agree with you. He should be tryna get to know you in every way possible," Ms. Maryanne said.

"Right, and he hated when I chose to do things with my mom instead of with him. I felt like he was jealous of our relationship."

"Yeah, that's how Andy is. He can be controlling at times, and he wants everything to be his way or no way. He's done that since we were kids," Gina told us.

"Wow," I said in disbelief.

After ranting about Andy and having small talk with Gina and Ms. Maryanne, I was on my way out the door. I was glad I'd come over to Gina's house. I got a chance to know them a little better. Gina was really nice, and she was very welcoming to Li'l T and me. I also got a chance to know the type of person Andy was, and still is.

I'm Over It

Li'l T and I were outside in our sweaters and hats. I sat on the porch as he ran through the yellow and orange leaves that fell onto the grass. Fall was definitely here. Thanksgiving was in just a couple weeks, and I was ready for it. I was very thankful for my family, but I was also thankful for the food that we eat during that time. As we were heading into the house, I received a phone call.

"Hello," I answered as I took off Li'l T's sweater.

"Hi, Keisha, how are you doing, dear?" asked Ms. Maryanne on the other end of the phone.

"I'm good. I just got in the house. Li'l T was out playing in the leaves." I smirked. "I'm about to put him in the bathtub. How are you doing?"

"I'm blessed. I just called to check up on you and also to invite you and Li'l T to Gina's house for Thanksgiving."

Not knowing how to answer, I paused. I'd never gone anywhere on Thanksgiving except to my mom's house.

"Unless you have other plans?" Ms. Maryanne asked.

"Um, no, no," I stuttered. "Well, I usually go to my mom's house for the holidays, but I'd love to come." I spoke halfheartedly.

"Wonderful. Well, I'll let you go so you can give Li'l T a bath. Give him a kiss for me. I love you all."

"We love you too," I said to Ms. Maryanne before hanging up.

My mind went to Andy. *Would he be there?* Since it had been so long since I'd heard from him, I didn't want it to be awkward, so I did what I hadn't done in a while. I called Andy. As I dialed his number, my heart raced a thousand beats per minute. I was relieved when the call went to his voicemail.

~ ~ ~

My cell phone rang. I'd been lying in bed for the past half hour, trying to convince myself to get up.

Still lying in bed, I answered the phone. "Hello."

"Happy Thanksgiving, Keisha," Ms. Maryanne yelled on the other end of the phone with great excitement.

"Happy Thanksgiving!" Hearing her joy brought a smile to my face. "How are you feeling today?"

"I'm good. How about you?"

"I'm blessed."

"Glad to hear that. We are going over Gina's house around two o'clock today so you can come over at that time if you would like to."

"OK, I'm going to my mom's house to hang out for a while, but I'll call you when I'm on my way over there later on this evening."

"OK, I will talk to you soon."

~ ~ ~

I spent the majority of the day at my mom's house. I was nervous about going over Gina's house because Thanksgiving is a huge family affair. I had only met Ms. Maryanne and Gina on Andy's side, and all I thought about was *Who was going to be there? What is the family like? What are their family dynamics? Will they like me? Will they welcome me into the family?*

It was six forty-five in the evening when I decided to leave my mom's house. It was seven when I arrived at Gina's house, and the driveway was full of cars. I started to get butterflies in my stomach. Although I knew Ms. Maryanne and Gina, I didn't know the rest of the family.

I sat in the car for ten minutes before I built up enough courage to knock on the door. As I was about to ring the doorbell, the door swung open.

"Hey, Keisha, Happy Thanksgiving!" said Gina with open arms.

"Happy Thanksgiving," I replied, escaping from her arms.

"Everyone is waiting to meet y'all," she said joyful. "We were wondering when y'all were going to show up."

"Well, I'm here now."

Gina picked up Li'l T and made her way to the kitchen, holding him in her arms. Li'l T hugged Gina's neck, seeming very comfortable around her. Knowing that, made me feel a little more at ease.

I followed her.

"Everybody, this is Keisha. Keisha, this is everybody." Everyone laughed.

"Hello, everyone, Happy Thanksgiving," I said, waving my hand from side to side.

"Happy Thanksgiving, Keisha, I'm your Uncle Seymore," a man said, walking towards me. He looked identical to Andy: same height, same weight, only his skin was two shades darker. "Come give me a hug, young lady. It is good to finally meet you. You are a beautiful young woman."

"Thank you," I said with a slight smile. "This is my son, Antavion, but we call him Li'l T."

"How are you doing, li'l man?" Seymore asked Li'l T, extending his right hand and waiting for Li'l T to do the same. "You wanna go play with the kids in the other room?"

"Yes, sir," Li'l T replied, holding onto Seymore's hand and walking with him, while I met other relatives.

"Hello, I'm your sister. My name is Dee-Dee."

"Hi, Dee-Dee. I'm Keisha," I replied. With light skin and long, curly, dark hair, Dee-Dee was gorgeous. She had big magnificent brown eyes, a nose just like mine, and was my height, but she was slimmer than I was. Her smile lit up the room as she showed off her pearly whites. She wore a nice red jumpsuit that fit her body perfectly and black high-heeled boots. She looked amazing.

"That is your other sister Candice," Dee-Dee said, pointing to a girl across the room. I couldn't tell how tall she was, since she was sitting down, but she appeared to be pregnant—like she might pop at any moment. She too was beautiful, with light skin and shoulder-length blond hair. She had nice full lips and a wide nose like we all had.

As I admired the beauty of my sisters, I heard a voice that I hadn't heard in over six months and I jumped, startled. It was Andy.

When he walked into the kitchen and noticed me, he looked shocked to see me standing there. But instead of saying anything to me, he brushed past me and walked towards the door.

"Wait!" I said as he made his exit. I followed him out the door.

He approached his car, his keys jangling in his hand.

"Andy!" I yelled.

He turned around. "What?" he replied nonchalantly.

At that moment, I became a mute. Then I forced myself to speak. "I-I was hoping that we could talk since we haven't spoken in months. I've called and texted you, but you haven't answered my calls or responded to my text."

"Yeah, honestly, I've been extremely busy lately." He looked at his phone.

"Too busy to even respond to my text?" I shouted. "I see you have your phone in your hand, and I know that people in fact do get busy, but not so busy that they can't even answer a text. People make time for what they want to make time for. You used to make time for me every day, even when you worked seven days a week!" I couldn't control my gestures. My hands were flying all over as I spoke. And I couldn't stop the annoyed expression on my face, or the tone of my voice. But he deserved to know how I felt. I was not sorry for expressing myself.

Andy's brows climbed up his head, a cocky expression on his face. "Yeah, you're right. Maybe I don't have time for you. Stop trying to call me, and please stop texting me! Matter of fact, just delete my number. No, better yet, I'll get my number changed!" He spoke aggressively. "I don't want anything to do with you! I fucked yo' mom one time, that's it!" he sliced his hand through the air with a note of finality. "You are not my daughter! Please just stay out of my life and stop coming around my family! You don't see me trying to get to know you, so why are you trying so hard? I have to go!" He got into his car and sped off.

My body became numb and my knees weakened. No man had ever spoken to me in such a way. I fell to my knees. My breathing became faster and faster, making it hard for me to catch my breath, and my heart pounded hard in my chest. Maybe my heart wanted to escape from my body and run away from me, just as Andy did.

I lifted my gaze to my surroundings. The bar trees swayed as the ground spun below me. Unable to remain upright on my knees, I allowed my body to collapse the rest of the way down. I felt like I was dying. And no one was around. I closed my eyes and thanked God for the life that I'd lived. Because I just knew this was the end of me.

~ ~ ~

A distant, urgent sound woke me. I opened my eyes, trying to figure out what made the noise. The sound came again, bringing me to full consciousness. I sat up. Why was I lying in a pile of leaves on the ground? I heard the noise again. I wiped my eyes and then realized it was the dog barking across the street behind the fence. I looked around to see where I was and suddenly, I felt the urge to throw up. And I did—all over Gina's lawn. I climbed to my feet and regained my balance, wondering what I'd been doing on the ground, outside in the cold with nobody around. After about a minute of being dumbfounded, I remembered the conversation that I'd had with Andy.

"I have to get outta here," I mumbled to myself.

I walked back into the house so that I could get Li'l T. Maybe if I acted as if I was interacting with people, then no one would notice when I left. I finally made my way to Li'l T. I gathered his things and headed for the door. Then I heard a voice call out.

"Keisha, are you leaving so soon?" Ms. Maryanne yelled.

"Yeah, I'm going to go ahead and go, not feeling so good, my stomach hurts"—not a lie; I'd just vomited in the yard—"but it's just cramps." OK, that was a lie.

"I wish you didn't have to leave so soon." Ms. Maryanne came close to me.

"I'll call you when I get home." I smiled and gave Ms. Maryanne a hug goodbye.

Then I picked up Li'l T and left without looking back. Once home, I tucked Li'l T into bed, then I cried like a baby. The pain was unreal, one of the worst I'd ever felt in my life. Not wanting anyone to bother me, I turned my cell phone off and unplugged my house phone. Lying in bed with my face in the pillow, I tried to wrap my mind around the situation, and I believed that Andy didn't mean anything he said.

I couldn't believe a man would say that to his daughter, the girl that he's supposed to love forever, the girl he's supposed to protect and look after. I felt like he'd ripped out my heart with his bare hands and stomped it to the ground. It might not have seemed like anything to him, but the words he spoke were words a daughter never wanted to hear her father say.

The next morning, I woke to Li'l T calling my name. I didn't sleep much at all, two hours total since we had gotten back from Gina's house.

I got myself together and made Li'l T some breakfast. I couldn't eat anything because I felt sick to my stomach from what went on last night with Andy. I couldn't hold onto this hurt for much longer. I had to look after Li'l T and I had to look after myself. While Li'l T enjoyed his breakfast, I turned my phone on and called my mom to see if she could look after him for a while.

"Sure, dear, that's no problem," Mom said over the phone. "I'm already out running errands, so I'll swing by in about twenty minutes."

After Li'l T left, I lay in bed and cried. I would not easily recover from this. Andy had given me the most devastating news I'd ever received. *How could a father say something like that to his daughter? What could I have done differently? Am I a bad daughter? What did I do to make everything go so wrong?* I questioned myself over and over.

Having been up for most of the night, I needed sleep so I went to the medicine cabinet in the bathroom, looking for the strongest thing that could knock me out. I found some Vicodin and popped three of them. I was not in any pain physically, but emotionally I was a wreck.

Sometime later, I woke up and looked at the clock. It was eleven a.m.

How could it have been eleven when my mom got Li'l T at noon? I turned on my cell phone and looked at the date. *Did I really sleep through an entire day?* I got up to use the restroom, looked in the mirror and cried. I didn't recognize the person looking back at me. I felt like *Helen Keller.* My eyes became unclear, and I could no longer see. My ears became blocked and I could no longer hear.

My stomach lurched. I spun to the toilet and spit up everything that was in me. It wasn't much, considering the fact that I hadn't eaten anything. After brushing my teeth, I lay back down and isolated myself from the world. No one could feel my pain. No one knew what I was going through. I slept another six hours before waking again.

Normally when things got bad for me, I'd turn to the Lord. The way I felt in this moment, I didn't want to pray. I didn't want to read the Bible. And I didn't want to go to church. As I was lying there feeling sorry for myself, I heard a voice say *Get Up*! I knew it was the voice of the Lord, so I became deaf to the voice, acting as if I hadn't heard it. Then the voice came again, and as much as I wanted to lie there and pity myself, I had to obey.

I rolled off the bed, dropped down to my knees and cried out to God. I became like Hannah when she prayed in her heart to the Lord to bless her with a son, my mouth moving but no words coming out. I opened my heart unto the Lord until I was able to speak. Then I spoke in my heavenly language until I felt my strength returning. I stood up sweating and feeling better than I had before I prayed.

There was something about calling on the name of Jesus. A person might feel a certain way before praying, but after calling on His name, that person will feel much better, no matter the situation. I turned on my gospel music and straightened up the house, singing praises unto His name.

Unknown Pain

Li'l T snuggled up with me on my bed, as the winter night winds blew. My cell phone lit up, indicating that I'd received a voicemail. I picked up my phone and found I'd missed a call from Ms. Maryanne. It had been a few weeks since I last talked to her. She'd been calling me, but I hadn't been answering the phone. I knew she hadn't done anything wrong, but I just didn't feel like speaking with her or anyone else on that side of the family. Pushing them away—especially Ms. Maryanne—wasn't right, but I didn't want them to invite me to anything else where I might run into Andy.

My cell rang. Ms. Maryanne calling again. I couldn't go on not talking to her; I'd grown to love her.

"Hello," I answered.

"Hey, Keisha, this is your grandma. I've been trying to get ahold of you. Is everything OK?" She sounded genuinely concerned.

"Yes, ma'am, everything is fine." I felt guilty lying to her.

"I'm so glad to hear that. I wanted to tell you about your father." She sounded disheartened. "I think you should go and see him."

"Go see him?" I repeated, shocked and annoyed. "I'm sure he wouldn't want to talk to me, let alone see me. Honestly, Ms. Maryanne, he's the reason I haven't been around and haven't been answering the phone. On Thanksgiving Day, Andy told me to stay out of his life and to stay away from all of you. I'm sorry that I haven't answered your calls, but now you know the reason why. I've been on an emotional rollercoaster, angry inside but also sad," I cried to Ms. Maryanne.

"Oh, sweetheart, I'm so sorry! I can't believe he told you that, Keisha." Her voice softened. "But on Thanksgiving Day, Andy was in a terrible car accident, and he's in a coma." Ms. Maryanne began crying on the other end of the phone.

"Oh, wow," I replied, not knowing how to react. A part of me wanted to say it was karma because of the way he'd treated me, but the other side of me was sad because he was still my father and knowing that he was in a coma grieved my heart. "What hospital is he at?" I asked.

"They had to life flight him to University."

"Oh, wow."

"Yeah, he was driving so fast and it was such a windy night that when he tried to stop, he swerved and hit a tree head on. Then a tree branch split in half and fell on the car. When they found him, he was unconscious. They had to pull him out of the car; it was so bad. He died twice before he got to the hospital, but they resuscitated him. He's lucky to be alive. I know it was nobody but God that kept him. Someone recorded it on their cell phone too, and I saw it."

"Oh, wow, that is crazy. I feel bad. I'm not sure if I can go see him just yet. I have so many emotions right now. I don't know what I should do."

"I understand, Keisha. I just wanted to make sure that you knew what had happen to him. Gina and I are going back up there in the morning, in case you want to go. I had been there since I got the call that he had died. The kids made me come home to shower and get some rest, but I haven't been able to sleep well, knowing that he's in the hospital helpless like that." Ms. Maryanne sobbed.

I could relate to her pain and anxiety. I remembered when the doctors told me that Li'l T wouldn't make it through the night. His tiny, lifeless body on a ventilator breathing for him because he was unable to do so on his own. It was by the grace of God that he was still here.

"If you need anything," I said, "please let me know. If I can do it, I will."

"OK, thank you, Keisha. I know what you can do for me."

"What's that?" I asked.

"Come with us to see your father. I know you feel some type of way right now, but maybe if you saw him, you'd feel differently."

"I don't know about that."

"It'll mean so much to me if you came along."

Because I genuinely cared for Ms. Maryanne, I found myself saying, "Ahh, well OK. But I'm only going as a support to you."

"Thank you so much, Keisha. I'm going to call Gina and tell her to make room for you because you're coming along with us to see your father."

"OK, I'll see you in the morning." I hung up the phone.

I lay there feeling an indescribable pain. I didn't want to go, but I'd told Ms. Maryanne I would. Not wanting to take Li'l T to the hospital, I called my mom so that he could spend the night with her.

~ ~ ~

The next morning, I woke up and got dressed so that I could go see Andy. Thirty minutes later, I was ready to go. I looked out the window, noticing the frost in the creases. Ten minutes later, a car horn sounded in the driveway. I went outside to find Gina, Ms. Maryanne, and Dee-Dee in the car.

"Hello, everyone." I slid into the back seat.

"Hey, Keisha," they replied in unison.

The drive to the hospital was quiet. I could tell everyone was sad and hurting, especially Dee-Dee. Her eyes were red, obviously from crying. When I first got into the car, I was filled with anxiety since I hadn't spoken to them since Thanksgiving. After a while, my nerves calmed down. Forty minutes later, we arrived at

University Hospital. As I stepped onto the elevator, my knees buckled and my head grew light. Luckily, only two people were allowed in the room at a time, so Ms. Maryanne and Dee-Dee had gone to see him first, while Gina and I found seats in the waiting room.

"Mama told me what Andy said to you. I don't know what's wrong with that man," Gina blurted, head shaking. "I couldn't believe he fixed his mouth to say something like that to you. I know he's fighting for his life right now, but sometimes my brother can be an asshole." She pursed her lips.

"Yeah, I didn't want to come at first, but I felt bad for Ms. Maryanne, and I wanted to be here for her."

"Yeah, I know. That's why I'm here. I feel so bad for Mama." Sitting with her forearms propped on the arm rests of her chair, Gina hung her head. "I know she's feeling sick about this. Growing up, Andy could get away with anything. He could murder someone in front of her, and she would still say he's innocent. That was her baby . . . and still is." Her tone held a hint of jealousy.

"Wow." I shook my head.

Dee-Dee came into the waiting room, and it was now my turn to go in. As I strode to the room, my heart beat faster and faster. I knew Andy was unconscious, but just remembering his harsh words to me made me not want to see him.

I entered the room and saw Andy lying helpless in a body cast. Ms. Maryanne sat in a chair by the window, her eyes on her son. I stepped closer to the bed, looked at him, and instantly burst into tears.

My reaction shocked me, but I no longer felt an unknown pain. I was hurt. I was sad. I was mad. I didn't want to see my dad lying there helpless.

Ms. Maryanne got up and strolled over to me, sobbing. She wrapped her arms around me and hugged me tight. I cried in her arms as if I was a small child, and she held me and told me that everything was going to be alright.

"I'm sorry, I'm sorry, I'm so sorry," I cried.

"What are you sorry for? You didn't do anything wrong, Keisha." Ms. Maryanne seemed to be trying to hold back her tears.

"It's all my fault," I cried. "I wanted him to talk to me so badly that I followed him outside Thanksgiving night. I wanted him to give me a reason for not responding to my text or answering my calls. That's when he told me to stay away from y'all and to stop calling and texting him." I cried harder than before.

"Keisha, sweetie, it's not your fault. Sometimes things just happen. Andy is going to be alright. I've been praying and praying for him, and I know the Lord heard my cry. He's gonna pull through. Just wait and see."

Soothed by her words and her confidence, I leaned into her hug and found peace.

Somehow it would be OK.

~ ~ ~

I was sitting in the chair next to Andy's bed, gazing outside as raindrops hit the windowsill. It had been almost two months since Andy's accident. I'd come up to the hospital every day since my first visit with Ms. Maryanne and Gina. Dee-Dee came with me at first, but then she stopped. She called me daily to learn his progress. He was doing better, but he still hadn't woken up from the coma.

Doctors said he should wake up any time, but we had to remember that everyone was different. I went down to the cafeteria for a snack, when I ran into an old friend.

"Keisha, what's up, girl? Is that you?" Hector Marrero, wearing a fresh white t-shirt and jeans, strutted toward me. While he dressed the same, he'd changed some since high school, lost weight and now sported a full, neatly trimmed beard. He wore his hair in a low-cut fade with waves. His smile—like a ray of sunshine—could brighten anyone's day.

"Yes, you know it's me," I said, returning the smile. As he drew near, I realized he now stood two inches taller than I did—and I had to admit homeboy was fine!—but I hadn't changed that much. "What's up? How have you been? It's been a while."

"I know, right?" he said with open arms. "I've been doing good. How you been, girl?"

"I'm good. I'm blessed by the best." I held onto him, feeling his back muscles and inhaling the fresh scent of his laundry detergent. I couldn't help but notice the smooth tone of his skin. Half Puerto Rican and half black, his skin was still two shades darker than mine.

"I hear that!" He pointed a finger up to the sky, smiling with his sexy brown eyes. "So, what you doing here?"

"My dad is here, up in ICU in a coma," I replied, downhearted, as my gaze shifted to the floor.

"Damn, I'm sorry to hear that, Keisha." He rested a hand on my shoulder. He'd always shown compassion toward others. He was one of the sweetest boys in my grade.

"It's cool, thanks."

"I didn't know you and your father were tight like that."

"Long story." I rolled my eyes. Hector and I used to talk a lot on the phone, back in high school. But he wouldn't realize that I'd recently developed a relationship with my father.

"Oh, OK. Well, is your number still the same?"

"Yes, it is."

"A'ight, girl, I'm gonna hit you up, if that's cool."

"Of course, it is." I gave him a warm smile.

"A'ight, girl, I'll see you later. And let me know if you need anything. I hope your dad pulls through."

"Thanks," I said to Hector before I walked away.

Hector

As I walked away from Hector, I thought about how long it'd been since we'd been in contact. It had been almost two years since he and I last talked. He used to call me every day around the same time when he got off work. I felt like I could tell him anything, and nothing I said would ever leave his mouth.

He made me feel so special with his words and always knew just what to say to me. Back then, I started to like him as more than just a friend. I didn't want to let him know because he and I were tight like that, and I didn't want to cross that line of being more than friends, so I slowly cut off communication with him. When he'd call me, I wouldn't answer the phone. Then eventually he stopped calling. I didn't want to lose focus on my walk with God, and I knew talking with someone often would only cause my focus to be elsewhere, especially if I was attracted to that person.

~ ~ ~

I walked off the elevator and down to Andy's room. I'd come up to the hospital every day for two whole months, and I hadn't prayed for him yet. I took his hand and prayed for him. *"Lord, watch over Andy!"* was all that I could say because the tears started rolling down my face, and I could no longer speak. So I let my heart speak for me. I rested my head on his hands and sobbed uncontrollably.

Suddenly, I felt movement. I lifted my head and looked down at his hands to be sure I wasn't trippin'. Andy's hands were really moving, and his eyes were creeping open.

"Nurse! Nurse!" I called out as I ran into the hallway as fast as I could.

Two nurses came rushing into the room. One told me to stand back as they took some vitals on him. I pulled out my cell phone and called Ms. Maryanne.

"Hey, Keisha, how are you?" Ms. Maryanne said.

"He's up, Andy woke up!" I shouted into the phone.

"Praise Jesus! Oh, thank you, Lord! Keisha, I'm going to call you back. I'm gonna call Gina and tell her to pick me up so that we can both come up there."

"OK, hurry." I hung up the phone with excitement.

After twenty minutes of examining Andy, the doctors and nurses left the room. He and I stared at each other face-to-face, but no one said a word.

"Hey." I finally broke the silence.

"Hey," Andy replied as a tear traced a path down his face.

"What's the matter?" I asked.

"I remember talking to you . . . Thanksgiving . . . then driving off, driving too fast. The weather was rough. Windy. What day is this?"

"Thanksgiving was over two months ago."

"Oh." He looked up at the ceiling as if thinking that over. Then he turned to me again. "I'm sorry for the things I said to you."

"It's OK. I forgive you. Let's not even talk about that now. I just want you to focus on getting better," I replied as my eyes welled with tears. Although I was hurt by what Andy had said to me on Thanksgiving, I had to move forward and not focus on that. It was a new year and I was going to leave the past in the past and focus on the future.

~ ~ ~

Ms. Maryanne and Gina were with Andy, so I decided to go home and see Li'l T. Since I'd been visiting Andy at the hospital, Li'l T's spent most of his time with my mom. I took him to Chuck-

E-Cheese so that he could have some fun. While we were there having fun, I ran into Hector again. He was there for his little cousin's birthday party. He came over and sat with me, and we watched Li'l T play on a trampoline full of balls. Hector and I laughed and talked just like old times.

I told him the situation with Andy, how he first came into my life and everything was great, and then how one day he told me to stay away. I really enjoyed talking with Hector. It brought back old memories that he and I shared. At the end of the evening, he and I promised that we'd keep in touch.

Rehabilitation

Andy and I sat in the room, watching the TV show *Blackish* as we waited for the nurse to transport him into another room. He'd been doing a lot better since last week when he woke up, so he was moved from ICU to the rehabilitation floor. He needed to regain his strength so the doctor thought it would be a good idea for him to be moved to rehab instead of sending him home right away. During the stay in rehab, Andy learned different exercises to regain his strength, and after two-and-a-half weeks of being there, he was ready to be discharged. The doctors told Andy that he shouldn't stay home by himself.

Andy asked if he could stay with me until the doctor cleared him for living on his own. No one in the family wanted Andy to stay with them, and Ms. Maryanne wouldn't be able to take care of him because she was getting up in age, so I agreed to let him come to my house until the doctor cleared him. During his stay with me, Andy stopped doing the exercises that physical therapy told him to do. I waited on him hand and foot. When he was hungry, I fed him. When he needed to be clean, I helped him washed up.

Whenever he needed anything, I was there for him. At times, I felt like I was a slave and he was my master. Ms. Maryanne and Dee-Dee called every day to check up on Andy and me, but no one ever offered to come over and help with him. I felt like no one really cared about him but me. I often looked at the situation as if it were me in his shoes. I would want someone taking care of me until I was able to get back on my feet.

I was falling behind on bills due to working less, and I had another mouth to feed. I had to care for a grown man, but he was my dad and I would do anything for him. He couldn't help me because he didn't have a job anymore, and he still had to pay the bills at his house.

"Hey, Andy, I'm gonna run to pay some bills. Do you think I can possibly not pay your cable bill so that I can pay on my light bill?" I asked sincerely.

"Well, I shouldn't be here much longer, and when I go home, I'm going to need something to watch. I'm sorry," he said with a shrug.

"It's OK," I assured him. "Do you think you could help get some food for the house? I've been trying my best to make sure we all eat and it's kinda hard for me."

Andy poked his lips out. "If you want me to leave, then I'll leave," Andy snapped. "All you have to do is tell me. I don't want to be somewhere where I'm not wanted."

"I never said I don't want you here. I only asked if you could help me out a bit." Lord knew I wanted to help him, but his attitude was very discourteous.

"Yeah, whatever." Andy threw up his hands.

"I'm basically your slave. I do everything for you! And you can't help me out?" My patience faded. "Maybe you SHOULD leave, because I can do bad by myself," I yelled.

"Fuck you!" Andy blurted out.

"Fuck me?" I repeated as I pointed to myself. "Really, Andy, there you go again, saying things out of your mouth. You better watch yourself!"

"What you gonna do?" Andy asked, testing me.

Without raising my voice and yelling back, I calmly responded, "It's time for you to go."

"OK, I'll go. Honestly, I don't need your help anymore either." Andy got up off the couch with no help and started to pack his things.

"So, you mean to tell me that you've been able to do for yourself this whole time?" I asked, the anger rising again.

"Yep," he replied nonchalantly. "It was nice being waited on hand and foot. Heck, I figured you owed it to me. After all the times I took you and Li'l T out and you didn't pay for anything, you owe me!" He gestured with his hands.

Tears filled my eyes. "I see why none of your family wanted to take you in. I was a fool to even let you in."

Andy didn't respond. He continued to pack his belongings into garbage bags. As he tied a bag, he yelled, "Stay out of my life!"

After filling two full trash bags, he stormed out and slammed the door behind him.

I didn't know who this man was, but this wasn't the guy that had tried to get to know Li'l T and me. *How could he be so harsh after I let him stay with me for almost two months?* I asked myself. I was happy Li'l T was with my mom and he didn't witness the madness.

~ ~ ~

Six o'clock at night, my phone rang, waking me from a nap on the couch. "Hello?" I answered, sounding groggy.

"What's up, girl? What you doing?" asked Hector.

"Not much. Just lying down." I sat up and pulled a soft throw over my legs.

"What's wrong, girl? Are you OK?"

"Yes, I'm fine. Me and Andy had a fight."

"Oh yeah? What about?"

"I'm falling behind on bills and you know I was taking care of him, so I asked if he could help me out. He basically said no and fuck you."

"Damn, I'm sorry to her that, Keisha. If you need anything, I got you," Hector replied.

"Thanks, but I'm good. I'll make it. I always do."

"Can I come over? I feel like I should be there with you."

"Yes, you can come."

"OK, I'll see you in a bit."

Fifteen minutes later, I opened the door and stood face-to-face with Hector. He walked into the house with his arms open, ready for me to embrace him. The fresh scent of his laundry detergent filled my nose. His embrace warmed me, and at that moment I felt a feeling that I haven't felt in over three years: he stirred feelings deep inside me.

"It's gonna be OK, girl." Hector released his arms from around me.

"It always is." I managed to smile.

"So, I'm here." He placed his hands on my shoulders. "What do you wanna do? Do you want to get out of the house and get some fresh air?"

"Honestly, I don't feel like going anywhere. I just want to chill out."

"OK, we can do that too. How about we order in and watch a movie?"

"Oh, so you tryna Netflix and chill, huh?" I said with a giggle.

He laughed too. "Nah, girl. I wouldn't do that to you. I'm just tryna get your mind off of the situation with your dad because I know how that is. I been there before. That shit hurts."

"Yes, it does," I replied.

We ordered pizza and watched the movie *Superbad,* starring Jonah Hill and Michael Cera. When the movie ended, Hector and I talked for hours. We laughed and joked around, and we listened to music. I introduced him to gospel music, which he'd never heard before.

"When T and I split up for good, I was so heartbroken even after everything he had put me through. This was the song that got me through. I had it on repeat, and I listened to it over and over." I put the cd into the cd player. We sat in silence as Yolanda Adams' song "Open My Heart" played in the background.

"That's a nice song," Hector said as the song ended.

"Yeah, I used to cry and sing at the same time. I felt like I was releasing some things if I sang along."

"I feel you, girl. I'm sorry that you had to go through all that shit with that nigga, and I'm sorry you're going through this shit with Andy. You don't deserve it." He took my hand.

"It's cool. I'm over T now." I shrugged my shoulders. "We all have to go through trials in life, some trials harder than others. I'm just happy I bounced back and didn't go crazy over T." I looked up and thanked God that I was still in my right mind despite what I'd been through with T.

"Fo' sho'. Ay, girl, it's past midnight, and you know I have to be up at five in the morning to go to work. I could talk to you all night, girl, but a nigga lightweight tired."

"Yeah, you've been talking for so long, I didn't want to say anything. I thought you were trying to avoid going home or something," I teased and then laughed.

He laughed too. "Oh, you got jokes, huh, girl? It's cool. Nah, but on some real shit, I really do enjoy talking with you and spending time with you, girl."

Hector looked me in the eyes, gazing at me as if I was the most beautiful woman in the world. For the first time in over three years, I wanted to kiss a man's lips, so I moved in closer to him as he stared.

"A'ight, girl, I'll text you when I get to the crib." He stood up from the couch and headed for the door.

"OK," I replied, feeling stupid. I'd thought at that moment that Hector and I were definitely going to have our first kiss, but I wrong. I walked him to the door and hugged him before he walked out.

One Wish

I stood up, singing along as the choir sung in praise and worship at church.

"Take ya time, Bishop!" Deacon Willie yelled as Bishop Bernard preached.

Bishop Bernard sure could preach! I loved hearing him speak. After church, Li'l T went home with my mom, since he was fussing to go with her. I went back home and started thinking about Andy. Even though I knew he wasn't thinking about me, I wanted to make sure he was doing OK. As much as his behavior hurt me, he was still my father.

Hector's ringtone, Ray J's song "One Wish," came through my phone, interrupting my thoughts.

"Hello," I answered.

"What's up, girl? What you doing?"

"Well, honestly, I'm glad you called because I found myself thinking about Andy."

"Man, fuck that nigga!" Hector said.

"Ha-ha-ha, right. What you up to?" I asked.

"Just got done smoking a blunt. I'm about to go and grab something to eat. You wanna roll with me?"

"Yeah, I'll be ready when you get here." The thought of seeing him excited me.

"A'ight."

After eating, Hector drove me back home and I invited him inside to chill. My feet ached, so I kicked my shoes off as soon as I came in the door. We watched the movie *The Eye,* starring

Jessica Alba. When the movie ended, we talked and laughed and joked like we always did.

As we sat there enjoying each other's company, I started rubbing the heel of one of my achy feet. Hector noticed so I felt the need to explain. "I wore high heels to church, trying to be cute, and my feet are still hurting." I laughed.

Instead of responding verbally, Hector scooted closer and grabbed my foot. He placed my left foot gently on his lap and massaged it.

His hands had a magic touch. "Ohhh, that feels so good," I moaned.

"I know," he muttered.

"Don't flatter yourself." I winked at him.

"Give me your other foot so that I can do that one too. You can't do one and not the other."

I did as I was told. After about a half hour of getting a great foot massage, it was almost ten o'clock at night.

"It's getting late, girl, I better get home."

"OK." I swung my feet to the floor and walked him to the door. "Call me when you get home."

"You know I will," he replied with open arms.

Hector hugged me as if this was the last time we'd see each other. I hadn't been with another man since T, and now three years later here with my friend Hector, I was very vulnerable. Hector must have been feeling the same way, because I felt his manhood rise onto my torso. My heart beat faster than a musician playing the drums on a Sunday morning while someone was dancing in the spirit. I looked Hector in the face and placed a soft kiss on his lips.

I wasn't surprised that he kissed me back. His lips felt good on mine as our tongues wrestled each other. His hands roamed my body stirring me up inside. Hector dropped to his knees and pulled up my skirt.

"GOODNIGHT!" I said sternly, tugging my skirt back in place.

"I'm sorry, girl." He backed up and got to his feet with his hands raised. "I thought you wanted me to."

"Oh, trust me, I do," I assured him. "But it's just—I don't know. I'll see you later. A'ight?"

"A'ight, Keisha, I hope you ain't mad at me. I would NEVER do anything to disrespect you or hurt you in any way." Hector's eyes held a look of regret and sadness.

"I know. It's not you; it's me. We good." I hugged him once again and kissed his lips. "We're good."

"OK."

Before Hector made it home, he texted me about ten times, apologizing if he disrespected me in any way. I tried my best to assure him that he hadn't.

~ ~ ~

The next morning, I woke up thinking about Hector. I couldn't help but think about him in every way, his touch, his kiss, his smell, his body, the way he looked at me and gave me his undivided attention . . . I didn't want to cross that line, because I didn't know what might happen between us and I didn't want to lose our friendship. *Should I call him? Wait, he's at work, maybe I'll text him. No, I'll just wait until he gets off work and calls me.*

After a day of chores and errands, I glanced at the clock. *Hector would soon call!* A moment later, my phone rang; Ray J's song played through my phone. *Finally!*

"Hello." I tried to sound casual, as if I hadn't been thinking about him all day.

"What's up, girl? What you doing?" Hector asked.

"Not much. Chilling. I just put Li'l T down for a nap. What you up to?"

"You know me; just lit this blunt."

"Right, I figured." Every day when Hector got home from work, he'd shower, smoke, and call me. "So, guess what?"

"What's that?"

"Honestly, I can't get you outta my mind. I keep thinking about what happen between us."

"Oh, yeah? Me too," Hector replied. Almost a minute went by and neither of us said a word.

"What if we became more than friends?" Nervous about his answer, I bit my lip.

"I mean, I like you, Keisha. You sexy as fuck, you easy to talk to, you have a good heart, any man would want to have a beautiful woman such as yourself in his corner, but I ain't tryna be in a relationship, plus I never had a girlfriend."

My heart sank. "Hector, let me call you back." I tried to sound as if my feelings hadn't gotten the best of me.

"I hope it's not something I said."

"Nah, you good," I lied before I hung up the phone, feeling disappointed. I wanted more than just a friendship with Hector, like I did before, but I had to respect his feelings.

~ ~ ~

I woke up the next morning to the sun peeking through my bedroom window, shining bright on my face. *Thank you, Lord, for another day,* I said silently to myself, smiling and looking up to heaven as I did each morning before I got outta bed.

"Li'l T, Li'l T, wake up, baby. We have to get ready for church," I whispered and kissed Li'l T on the cheeks. I could tell he was already awake because he opened his eyes and closed them again, smiling. "Well, I guess I will get ready for church and let Li'l T stay here all by himself since he is still sleeping," I joked.

"I'm not sleeping, Mommy, I tricked you." Li'l T laughed.

"You did! I'm gonna get you." I tickled him all over, and he laughed even harder.

After playing around, we got ready for church. When we arrived, I took Li'l T to the children's class and then I sat in the adult class.

"Touch your neighbor and say, 'Neighbor, God is good all the time, and all the time, God is good.'" Bishop Bernard yelled over the podium as he preached. "While your tryna figure it out, He's already worked it out."

The saints at church responded by shouting, "Hallelujah" and "Amen."

"I dare about nine of you to jump up and turn around and say, 'It's already done,'" Bishop Bernard said through the microphone.

Everyone turned around, and half of the saints started dancing in the spirit of the Lord. I loved church service when the spirit was high. It let me know that God was in the place and that He could turn my situation around. When church was over, Li'l T and I went to my mom's house so that we could have Sunday dinner with them. On the drive there, I received a phone call.

"What's up, girl? What you doing?" asked Hector.

"On my way to my mom's house to eat with them. We just got outta church. What's up with you?"

"Not much. Watching the game. How was church?"

"Church was great! Bishop Bernard preached a good message. We have evening service at five. Would you like to come with us?" I asked, hoping he'd say yes.

"Um, I ain't been to church in a minute, girl, plus I just got done smoking a blunt."

"What does that mean?" I asked. "God sees all, and He knows all."

"Yeah, you right." He paused. "OK, I'll go with you."

"OK, great! I'll pick you up around four thirty. I'll text you before I leave my mom's house."

"A'ight, girl," Hector said before he hung up.

~ ~ ~

During service, I looked over at Hector and noticed a tear fall from his eyes. I didn't say anything about it. Instead I leaned closer to him and grabbed his hand and smiled.

"Did you enjoy yourself?" I asked Hector on the way back from evening service.

"Yes, I did," Hector replied. "I don't know why my eyes were watering while the preacher was preaching."

I laughed. "Boy, stop! You know yo' eyes were not just watering." I playfully punched him in the arm.

"I'm not sure what it was."

"It was the spirit of God." I smiled.

"What do you mean?" he asked, his expression showing that he waited with bated breath.

"Well, I'm no preacher, but the spirit is something that you can't explain, but you just *know*. The spirit hits everyone differently. Some people by crying, some people dancing, some shouting. It just depends." I tried my best to put it into words. "Maybe you could go back with us sometimes and also come to a few Bible study classes. Bishop Bernard can and will explain things to you. He can break it down so that you can get a better understanding."

"I don't know, girl."

"It won't hurt anything, Hector!"

"A'ight, girl, for sure. I'll go with you."

Without replying, I continued to drive and pray silently in my head. We were all God's people, and He wanted us to go out and minister to different people that might not look like we do.

<h1 style="text-align:center;">Official</h1>

The ringing of my cell phone interrupted a dream about me and Hector. In the dream, we were at my house, and to my surprise we made love to each other as we listened to *R. Kelly* playing in the background.

"Hello," I answered not fully awake, wanting to get back to my dream.

"Good morning, sleepy head. I was just calling to make sure that you were awake for church."

"Good morning to you too." I smiled, realizing that it was just the person that I had been dreaming about. "Yes, I'm awake."

"OK, well get ready, because I will be there soon, girl."

"OK, see you soon."

"A'ight, girl."

I got out of bed and thanked God for another day, but I also had to repent because of the dream I'd had about Hector. It had been two months since Hector first started going to church with me. He'd gone to church with me every Sunday since. He'd come to my house and pick up me and Li'l T, and we'd head to church as if we were a family.

The more Hector came, the more he participated in church, standing up and singing along to praise and worship. He had even started paying his tithes to the church. After church was over, we pulled up at my house, but we didn't get out the car just yet because we were listening to "Greater is Coming" by Jekalyn Carr. We sang along and talked about how good the song was. We also talked about us.

"I don't want you to take this the wrong way, but I'm really starting to like you," I whispered to Hector so that I wouldn't wake up Li'l T as he slept in my arms. He had climbed up to the front seat while we were listening to music and singing along.

"I'm starting to really like you too, Kiesha." Hector looked directly into my eyes, giving me his undivided attention. "I love how we vibe, and I love the chemistry that we have. Because of you, I've changed some of my ways for the better, I don't smoke as much as I used to. I don't cuss as much, so I want to thank you for that."

"Well, don't thank me. Thank God."

"Of course, I thank Him." He smiled. "But He placed you in my life, so I thank Him each day for you as well."

I smiled at him, and at that moment I became nervous, and my hands sweaty. Hector and I had been hanging out a lot, but I felt awkward in the moment.

"I thank God for you too," I said. "Well, when are we gonna stop playing and make it happen?" I spoke up, shocked at the words that came out of my mouth.

"Now." Hector spoke still gazing into my eyes.

I was shocked at his reaction; I repeated him.

"Now?" I placed my hand on my chest.

"Yes."

"So, what does that mean, now? Are you officially my man?" I asked anxiously.

"Yes." Hector smiled as he grabbed my chin and leaned in closer to me. He placed a gentle kiss on my lips, his gaze never leaving my eyes.

I stared at him with amazement and kissed him back.

~ ~ ~

Hector's and my relationship moved rather quickly. He and I were the perfect couple. We did a lot of things together. We often wrote poems to each other, and sometimes we'd write them together. My feelings for him were blossoming into love. I didn't know how to tell him, because I thought it might have been too soon since we'd only been officially together for three months.

~ ~ ~

My mom, Li'l T, and I sat outside on her porch, enjoying the warm summer air, when an unfamiliar car pulled into her driveway.

"Who is that?" I asked my mom, confused.

"I don't know," she replied, just as confused as I was.

"What's up, y'all?" T said as he got out the car.

I instantly caught an attitude. T hadn't been around in three years, and now he wanted to show his face?

"What are you doing here?" I said, anger bubbling up.

"I can't come and see my son?" T smiled at me, licking his lips.

"Oh, it's nice to know that you now remember you have a son! Wow! How long did it take you to realize that?" I said sarcastically.

"Keisha, if he wants to see Li'l T, just let him do it without you jumping down his back," my mom said to me.

"Ugh." I growled as I got up and walked into the house. I couldn't believe my mom took his side and not mine.

Minutes later, T walked into the house and found me in the living room.

"Can we talk?" he asked, standing over me.

"About what?" I said with an attitude as I flipped through the TV channels, never taking my eyes off the screen.

"Why are you upset with me? I came to see our son," he said nonchalantly.

I was angry that T fixed his mouth to say the words "our son." *How dare he say it's his son when he doesn't do anything for Li'l T, nor does he call to check up on him.*

"You came to see 'our son' but yet you're in here with me. Go outside and see MY son and leave me alone."

Ignoring what I said to him, T smiled and licked his lips once again. "You looking good, Kesh."

"Well, it's probably because I have a boyfriend that cares for me," I said with a grin.

T's smile vanished. "How long have y'all been together?"

"Why?" I replied, my attitude never leaving.

"Because, I wanna know."

I didn't reply.

"I miss you, Keisha. I've been thinking a lot about you lately."

I'm sure the only reason you "claim" to be thinking about me is because I have a boyfriend, I thought to myself.

"Boy, bye! How long has it been since I saw you? Instead of thinking about me, you should be thinking about your son." I rolled my eyes.

"I do think about him. Do you think we can make this thing work and be a family like you wanted before?" T sat down beside me.

"Ha-ha, T, you're funny." I got up off the couch and walked away.

"Keisha, baby, I love you!" He stood in front of me, grabbed my hand and looked into my eyes. "I'm sorry about everything that I put you through in the past. I know I messed up a lot, but I am a changed man now. I'm tryna do the right thing. And if you give me another chance, you will see that."

T saying those words to me brought back memories. He and I shared good memories, when he wasn't being a jerk to me.

"Do you think we can take a ride real quick?" T asked me.

"Where to and why?" I folded my arms across my chest and gave him a stern look.

"Because I want to show you something."

"Show me what, boy?" I replied to him aggressively.

"Just come on. Please!" he said with a look that evoked pity.

In that moment, I felt sorry for T. Just like back then, T had a way of getting to me and making things go his way. I followed T out the door. We took a drive and ended up at the lake. We used to go to the lake often and watch the sunset, and just gaze at the water and talk about everything on our minds at that time.

"T, why are we here?" I asked, my arms still folded across my chest.

"I just want to talk. I heard you met your dad. How did that go?"

"How do you even know that?" I poked my lips out, waiting for an answer.

"I got my connections. I know you've always wanted to meet him, so I just wanted to know how that went."

"Well, yes, I met him, and that was that. Nothing else to it." I rolled my eyes for the third time. "Why are you stalking me anyways?"

"I'm not stalking you. You were on my mind, and I was asking about you. I heard you go to church a lot too. That's what's up. Remember when we use to go to church together?" he asked, reminiscing about the past.

"T, take me back to my mom's house! There's no reason for you to be asking around about me. I'm not your girlfriend, and you don't need to keep tabs on me!"

"Keisha, I love you, and I want us to be together again. You have my firstborn, and I want to be with you."

"Boy, like I said, you can take me back to my mom's house. I'm cool on you. I'm not sure why I even took a ride with you in the first place."

Without replying, T lunged toward me and kissed me on the lips.

It had been three years since T and I had any kind of interaction with each other. I didn't know how or what I should be feeling. T placed his hand on my thigh and worked his way up. I felt numb. Here I was allowing the person who had hurt me the most in my life touch me in a way that he shouldn't. My heart was no longer with T anymore. I'd moved on with my life, and I had a new man. T was not in my future.

I turned away, breaking his kiss, and pried his hand off my leg. "T, get up and get off me. I can't do this."

"Yuck!" I wiped my mouth with the back of my hand.

"Look, I got a man, and I don't want to hurt him because I love him." I shoved him away from me.

"You love him?" T yelled.

"Yes, I do. He respects me, and he treats Li'l T as if he was his own. I can honestly say that my heart is no longer with you." I finally spoke calmly.

"How do you know that?"

"Because I know. I'm mad that I allowed you to kiss me." I pulled the neckline of my shirt up and wiped my mouth again. "I won't keep you away from Li'l T, if you are serious about being in his life this time. You're welcome to see him anytime you want. Now can you please take me back to my mom's?"

"But, baby, I love you. I'm so sorry for everything." T spoke sympathetically.

"How about a round of applause?" I clapped my hands. *"And don't tell me you're sorry, 'cause you're not. Baby, when I know you're only sorry you got caught, but you put on quite a show. You really had me going, that was quite a show, but it's over now."* I sang Rihanna's "Take a bow."

"Oh, it's like that?" T asked.

"I forgive you, T, and I accept your apology." I smiled and got out of the car. "Oh, yeah, one more thing . . . Thanks!"

"Thanks, for what?" T asked.

"I'm thanking you for everything that you've done to me. Not only have you changed, but so did I. I am a much stronger woman than I was back then. I have more respect for myself now. But I wish you all the best of luck, T, I really do. I will always love you in a godly way because you gave me the most precious gift a woman could ever have, so I also thank you for that." I wiped the tears from my eyes.

Then I flipped my middle finger, and my index finger followed. I gave T the deuces and walked away. Feeling good about how I'd handled things, I sat down on the bench and gazed out at the water before I called my mom to pick me up.

~ ~ ~

I had just finished giving Li'l T a bath because he had gotten dirty while we were at my mom's house. As I was laying out his clothes, my phone rang.

"Hello," I answered as I put Li'l T's shirt over his head.

"Hey, baby, what you doing?" Hector said on the other end of the phone.

"Just finished giving Li'l T a bath, and now I am about to fry some chicken. What did you eat for your lunch break?" I asked.

"Mom made some pork and rice and beans. I just got done eating that."

"Oh, OK. Do you want me to save you some chicken for when you get off?"

"Nah, baby, I'm cool. I'm full off that! Anyways, I miss you, girl."

Whenever Hector told me that he missed me, it made me feel special and I got to the point that I couldn't stop smiling. I still got butterflies when he called me, as if we'd just met for the first time.

"I miss you too, boo." I stopped in my tracks and smiled uncontrollably. "I can't wait to kiss your lips when you get off of work."

"Me too. Are you gonna wear something sexy for me?" Hector asked. He and I would often play around as if we were going to have sexual intercourse, but we never took it to the next level.

"I don't know. I might." I smiled from ear to ear. I loved Hector, and I would do anything to make him happy.

"Honestly, girl, you don't have to have on anything because you're sexy enough for me."

"And you know this, man," I replied as if I was Smokey from the movie *Friday*.

He laughed. "You're so silly, baby. A'ight, look, baby, I'm about to go clock back in, so I will see you in a li'l bit. I love you, girl."

"I love you too, papi." I hung up the phone to make dinner.

Hector and I had been together for six months now. He worked on weekdays and stayed at my house every night. On the weekends, his days off, my mom would watch Li'l T, and he and I would go on dates or do something fun to enjoy each other.

Holiday Cheer

Hector and I sat on the couch and silently watched the competition television show *Sunday's Best* on BET, as we did each Sunday during the season. It was almost Christmas time, and I had a lot of shopping to do for my family—as well as for Hector. Nine months had passed since we'd been together, and I loved Hector more and more each day. The temptation was beginning to get to me, and I could no longer hold off. I wanted to take it to the next level with him, and since Christmas was coming up, I figured that would be a great present to give to him.

"What do you want for Christmas, girl?" Hector asked during a commercial break.

"Umm, I don't know, boo." I shrugged my shoulders. "I will be happy with whatever you get me." I smiled.

"How about I wrap myself up?" he winked at me.

"Well, since I already got you, I was thinking something else."

Hector didn't reply. Instead, he took me into his arms and kissed me passionately. Li'l T stayed the night with my mom, so Hector and I were all alone.

"Let's go to the store after the show," he said. "I liked the necklace that you got your mom for Christmas, and I wanna get my mom one too."

"OK." I rested my head on his shoulder and faced the TV.

After *Sunday's Best* ended, we headed to the store and decided on the necklace that Hector was going to get his mom. I continued to browse around the jewelry store. As I glanced around, a special ring stood out. It was a beautiful heart-shaped, fourteen karat gold ring with diamonds set in a cross inside the heart. *I love this.*

Hector must've noticed me gawking at the ring, because he came over to me. "You like that, girl?" he asked as the ring also caught his attention.

"Yes, it's beautiful." My eyes never left the ring.

"Well, too bad I already got you something, or else I'd get it for you." Hector smiled.

Without replying, I folded my arms and walked away, heading for the door. He followed me out.

~ ~ ~

On Christmas Eve I sat downstairs on the couch, watching the Christmas tree as the lights blinked on and off. It was ten o'clock at night, and Hector and Li'l T were already asleep upstairs after watching reruns of the 1983 movie *A Christmas Story*. I was awake, thinking about how blessed I was. I had a wonderful son, and I had a great boyfriend that treated me with the respect that I deserved. Life couldn't get any better. After thirty minutes of being in my thoughts, I went upstairs and snuggled up next to Hector in bed.

~ ~ ~

"Mommy, Mommy, wake up!" Li'l T yelled as he jumped up and down on my bed.

"Babe, wake up. It's Christmas!" Hector kissed me on the lips.

I opened my eyes. Hector and Li'l T were jumping up and down, insisting that I wake up. I couldn't help but smile, because my two favorite people were here with me on Christmas morning.

"Mommy, I got you something," Li'l T commented enthusiastically.

"You did? What did you get me, baby?" I loved seeing my son so happy. His happiness meant the world to me.

Without replying, Li'l T ran into his room. He returned with a homemade card that read *Merry Christmas to the bestest mommy in the world. I love u!*

"Aw, baby, this is beautiful." My eyes became watery. "Did Hector help you make this?"

"Yes, ma'am," Li'l T replied, smiling and showing his teeth, except for the two fronts that had already fallen out.

I loved the way Hector was with Li'l T. Little things like this made me appreciate him even more.

"This is from me, babe." Hector gave me a card along with a small box.

This has got to be the ring that I was looking at, I said to myself. I opened the box and found a pair of round, gold diamond earrings.

"Aw, boo, these are beautiful." I watched them sparkle in the light. While it wasn't exactly what I wanted, it still had diamonds, so I was fine with it. "I love you, babe." I hugged and kissed him.

"I love you too, girl. Come on. Let's go downstairs. I got you something else, plus we wanna open our gifts too," Hector said with a smile.

As we walked downstairs, I noticed a fifty-inch flat screen TV mounted on the wall. It was the same TV that I was looking at when we went to the store last month.

"Aw, babe, you didn't have to get the TV. I was going to get it when I got my tax refund. How'd you even know that I wanted it?"

"I know everything, girl. It's my job to know things that you like and things that you don't like. I remembered when we went to the store, you was looking at this. I know you didn't say anything to me about it, but I know how you are; when you want something, you look at it for a while and then you'll go back and get it."

I didn't reply to Hector. I just kissed him on the lips.

"Mommy, I wanna open the big one." Li'l T interrupted our kiss.

"OK, baby, let me get my camera first so that I can record you, and we could show grandma when we get to her house."

After Li'l T opened his presents, we cleaned up the living room and got dressed so that we could head to my mom's. Hector and I were gonna meet up later; he wanted to spend some time with his mom. After Li'l T opened his presents at my mom's house, we ate. Then I took a nap and woke up and ate again. It was getting late, so after saying my goodbyes to my family, I headed home. My mom wanted Li'l T to stay the night and he didn't put up a fight, so I let him stay.

"Hey, babe, where you at?" I called Hector on the drive home.

"Waiting for you to get home so that I can come over and give you something else."

"Oh, really, and what is that?" I asked curiously.

"You gotta wait and see."

"Well, I'm on my way home now. Don't meet me there, beat me there."

"OK, babe, I'm leaving now. I love you."

"I love you too, babe." I hung up the phone. I couldn't wait to see Hector. Even though I woke up to him, it felt like forever since I had seen him, and I couldn't wait to see what else he had for me. *He's probably really going to wrap himself up.* I knew just how silly Hector was. Fifteen minutes later, Hector and I pulled up at my house at the same time.

"I said beat me here, not meet me here," I joked as I got out of the car.

"But I'm here, and that's all that should matter." Hector stood face-to-face with me in the driveway.

"You right. I missed you so much," I said, biting my bottom lip because Hector was one sexy man.

"I missed you too, girl." He wrapped his arms around me and kissed me on the lips.

We walked into the house and he French kissed me, not allowing me to close the door behind me.

"So, is this what else you had for me?" I asked in between kisses.

"You already know, girl." He kissed my neck.

"Let me go freshen up. I've been in these clothes all day." I wanted to slip into my new Christmas lingerie that I had bought especially for this occasion. He had no idea what was in store for him tonight.

"A'ight, girl, hurry up."

When I got out of the shower, Hector was stretched out on the bed half asleep. I climbed into the bed next to him and kissed him on the lips.

"How was your shower?" Hector asked as he got up off the bed and turned the light on, noticing what I was wearing.

"It was nice." I spun around so that he could get a better view of me.

"Damn, girl! You sexy as hell! I wasn't ready for that." He licked his lips in a seductive manner. "Are you sure you want to do this?" Hector asked hesitantly.

Instead of replying, I nodded my head yes, and our souls became intertwined for the first time that night.

~ ~ ~

"I love you, girl." Hector kissed my forehead as I lay on his bare chest.

"I love you too, Big Daddy," I responded.

"What time is it?"

"I don't know. Why are you worried about the time?" I asked, curious to know why the time was so important to him now, in this moment.

"I told you I had something else for you."

Hector got up from the bed, reached into the closet and pulled out another small box.

"Um, what is that?" I asked with a look of confusion.

"Open it." He handed me the box.

I opened the box and found the ring with the heart and the cross inside. I was astonished! I sat there with my mouth open until I felt my eyes starting to water.

"Aw, babe. When di—"

"Shhh." He cut me off. "So I take it that you like it?"

"Babe, I LOVE it. I love you so much, Big Daddy. You mean so much to me. I'm so happy to have you in my life; I've been through a lot in my past relationships. I didn't think there were good men out here. I thought all men were liars and cheaters, but you're showing me different, babe, and I love you so much for that. I think this is why God allowed us to be together, so that you could show me how a man is supposed to treat his woman. There's more to it than the ring, babe. It's how you are with Li'l T. And how you tell me I'm beautiful every day. Your actions speak louder than your words." I cried.

"Babe, you don't ever have to worry about me cheating or lying to you. I love you; you're my first girlfriend and hopefully my last. I tell you you're beautiful because you are. As a matter of fact, you sexy as hell. The first day I seen you, I wanted you, and not in a sexual way either. I knew there was something different about you, girl. Hopefully, one day you'll be more than just my girl."

I couldn't respond. All I could do was cry. I loved him so much. That night we made love until the sun came up, and he was no longer Hector to me. He was now Big Daddy.

New Year

I lay in bed as the sun peeked through the bedroom window, shining bright on my face. Big Daddy and I made love all night. We became magnets for each other.

"Good morning, girl," Big Daddy said, kissing my lips.

"Good morning, Big Daddy. What time is it?" I replied.

"It's almost noon."

"Oh my," I said, yawning.

"You had a nigga up all night, girl. We just went to sleep at seven this morning. I wasn't expecting the night to go down like that at all. But I loved every bit of it, and I love every bit of you too, girl." He gazed into my eyes, giving me his full attention.

"I love you too, Big Daddy." I kissed his lips.

"Get up. I made breakfast." Big Daddy walked downstairs.

After taking a shower, I went to the kitchen for breakfast. The thought of Andy crossed my mind; he was the last person to make a big breakfast in my kitchen. I wondered how he was doing. At times, I missed the moments Andy and I spent together, even though our relationship had been short-lived. Since Big Daddy and I had been together, I rarely thought about Andy, and when I did, Big Daddy always did something to redirect my mind without even knowing what I was thinking.

"OMG!" I said with my mouth wide open. "Babe, you didn't have to do this." He'd prepared a romantic breakfast, setting the table for two with red roses spread across it. In the middle sat a small fruit dish of pineapple and grapes—my favorites. Next, he had a bottle of Mimosa chilling on ice and two glasses filled with orange juice.

"Right this way, miss." Big Daddy grabbed my hand and led me to my seat. When he pulled out my chair, I found a small stuffed animal that said I love you.

"Aw, babe. I love you." I stared into Big Daddy's eyes.

Big Daddy didn't reply. Instead he kissed my cheek and pushed my chair in. "Are you ready to be served, Miss Lady?"

"Yes," I answered with a smile.

Big Daddy lifted the stainless-steel cloche, revealing two heart-shaped pancakes and bacon that spelled out "I love you."

"Aw, babe. How'd I get so lucky to have you?" I asked Big Daddy.

"Nah, girl. How did 'I' get so lucky to have you?"

"You make me fall in love with you more and more each day."

"That's the plan. I'm already in love with you, girl. I'd do anything to keep you smiling," Big Daddy said. "I wrote something for you, girl. It's called 'Wonderful.' Wonderful is you, wonderful is we, together forever, the way it's gonna be. I love your touch, your kiss, I just love the way you make me feel, baby, I'm for real. You my boo today, tomorrow, and every day, and that's the way it will remain," Big Daddy freestyled.

"OMG, babe, I love it!" Tears filled my eyes.

Is this for real? How did I get so lucky as to end up with a guy like him? Thank you, Lord, for sending him to me, I silently prayed. *After the men I've been with in my past and all the mistakes I've made in my life, I finally have someone that not only tells me that he loves me, but also shows me. And I know in my heart that he's for real. Lord, I just wanna say thank you for everything that you have done for me, because you didn't have to do it, but I'm glad you did. And for that I say thank you.*

~ ~ ~

A week later, Hector and I had fallen deeper in love. I woke up around one in the morning with a lot on my mind. I lay in Big Daddy's arms and thought about how I needed to change.

"Big Daddy, are you sleep?" I asked.

"Halfway. Why, what's up?" He sounded concerned.

"I've been thinking, babe . . . I love you so much, but this just doesn't feel right."

"What you talking about, girl? What don't feel right?" Big Daddy sat up in bed.

I sat up too. "This . . . us."

"Keisha, you're not explaining yourself well. What are you talking about?" He sounded a bit frustrated.

"Baby,"—I took his hand— "I love you, but what we're doing just doesn't seem right. We've been going to church a lot, and I've been listening to Bishop Bernard, and it feels like I'm living in sin. Babe, we're not married, but we do things as if we were. I just don't feel like we should be doing this, sleeping together, making love." I spoke from my heart. "In marriage, couples give themselves to each other completely, exclusively, and forever, with a love that creates—the way God's love creates."

Bishop Bernard's words over the years, his messages on marriage, came to me. "Bishop Bernard says marriage is a symbol of the love Christ has for His Church, His bride. Jesus gives Himself completely and forever for His Bride, don't you see? So"—I struggled to put my thoughts into words—"sexual intimacy is the body language of married love. You know what I'm saying? Outside of marriage, it's really a lie. The unmarried couple hasn't promised themselves forever and exclusively to each other."

"And they aren't usually open to the life that lovemaking creates. I guess that's why we know . . . people instinctively know sex outside of marriage is wrong. It's really just selfish pleasure, even when one feels they love the other. The promises exchanged in marriage . . . they change everything, you feel me?"

"Damn, girl, that was deep." He rested his hands on the top of his head. "I'm not sure how to respond to that." He rubbed his head. "I thought you were breaking up with me, girl." He laughed, sounding relieved. "But I love you too, girl. I kinda been thinking the same thing, but then when I get next to you and feel your soft body next to mine, I have a change of heart."

"You've been thinking that too?" I was surprised. "Well, I wanna start the New Year off by not having sex. What do you think about that?"

He gave me a flustered look before he spoke up. "OK, we can do that." He shrugged his shoulders. "You made me wait before, so I will wait again. But as for now, how about we go one last time? How about I take yo panties off and go deep sea diving?"

Without waiting for me to respond, Big Daddy went under the covers and did what he does best. We made love like we did our first time, only this time it was better. I loved him so much. I could see myself spending the rest of my life with him.

~ ~ ~

I was in the mirror setting my face, doing the finishing touches to my make-up as I got ready for church. Big Daddy and Li'l T had been dressed and ready for twenty minutes already.

"Babe, are you ready yet?" Big Daddy yelled up the stairs for the third time. "It's New Year's Eve. You know church is going to be packed. We have to go."

"Yes! I'm almost done. Give me a minute," I yelled back.

Ten minutes went by, and I was all ready to go. We pulled up into the church parking lot, where cars were lined up in the grass.

"Oh, I didn't know church was going to be this packed," I said.

"Yeah, somebody took their time getting ready, but I won't say no names," Big Daddy said sarcastically, looking in my direction.

"Shut up." I playfully punched him in the arm.

We walked into the crowded church as they were singing praise and worship. We weren't able to sit in our usual seats because they were already occupied, so we sat two rows back and joined in as the choir sang. After the choir sang, it was now time for Bishop Bernard to bring the word of God.

"You've completed some things in 2017, but in 2018 you're walking into your New!" Bishop Bernard said as his closing statement. "Give your neighbor a hug and say, 'Happy New Year.'" Bishop wiped the sweat from his face and went over and hugged his wife.

Big Daddy and I hugged, and I cried in his arms. It was a new beginning for us, and new things were going to start to fall in place for us. I felt it.

New Beginnings

I sat at my desk at work, reminiscing on how I got to where I am. *God has truly blessed me,* I told myself. Two years ago, after I had received my high school diploma, I had taken some online classes. One of the classes was Medical Terminology, and I received my completion certificate within weeks. I finally put it to use six weeks ago when I had received a job as a receptionist at a dermatologist's office.

"Are you feeling OK, Keisha?" asked Jenny, my boss.

Jenny was a petite, middle-aged Caucasian woman that was built like most of the women on today's reality TV shows, only Jenny didn't pay for hers. She worked out five to six days a week to keep her body in shape. If you asked me, she was built like Jennifer Lopez, but better. Before I came along, Jenny had tried to do everything on her own ever since she'd opened her own practice. During the six weeks that I'd been working, Jenny and I had become close.

One day, I was praying in the breakroom and Jenny walked in. She noticed I was praying and asked if I could pray for her. From that day on, Jenny and I prayed each morning before we opened up.

"Yes, I'm fine." I lied. "I just have to use the restroom. I've been feeling nauseous lately."

"Are you pregnant?" Jenny asked.

"No!" I blurted out.

"Well, have you taken a test? I haven't said anything, but I've noticed that you've been using the restroom more often too. Have you gotten your period?"

"No," I answered, realizing that Big Daddy and I haven't been quite as sexually abstinent as we had planned on being.

During my lunch break, I went out and got a pregnancy test, but I was hesitant to take it. *What if I'm pregnant? What will I do with a baby right now? I'm not married!? What will people think of me? I can't have another baby out of wedlock!* I questioned myself, allowing my thoughts to get the best of me. After thirty minutes of letting my mind wonder, I finally built up enough courage to take the test, but then I couldn't bring myself to read the results.

"Jenny!" I yelled.

"Are you OK?" Jenny rushed into the restroom and came up beside me.

"Would you read the test for me? I just can't." I put my head down.

"Of course, I can." Jenny grabbed the stick from my hand.

"Well, congratulations, Keisha, you're pregnant!" she yelled with much exhilaration.

Instead of sharing in her joy, I burst into tears. "How did this happen?"

"Well, I'm sure you know how it happened." Jenny laughed. "Why don't you take the rest of the day off, and I'll finish up here."

"OK."

There were so many emotions going through my head. I called Big Daddy and told him that I was leaving work because I wasn't feeling well. I left out the part that I had taken a pregnancy test. When I arrived at home, Big Daddy had a nice warm bath ready for me with rose pedals around the tub. While I bathed, he made me some soup and got the bed ready for me. After I ate, Big Daddy gave me the best foot massage ever.

"OK, Big Daddy, so what's the catch? I'm not giving you none of this good, good." I laughed.

"There is no catch when it comes to you, girl. I'll do anything to make you happy and to see you smile." He stared at me with his sexy brown eyes.

"You always know what to say to make me smile."

"And that's how I want to keep it, girl. Now lay down and get some rest. I'll be here if you need anything." Big Daddy pulled the blanket over me and tucked me in as if I were a child.

"Wonderful is you," he spoke.

"Wonderful is we," I spoke.

"Together forever, the way it's gonna be. I love your touch, your kiss, I just love the way you make me feel, baby, I'm for real. You my boo today, tomorrow, and every day, and that's the way it will remain." We quoted *Wonderful* together in unison.

Surprise

I lay on the couch with Li'l T, watching *Peppa Pig*. He laughed every time one of them snorted. I loved seeing Li'l T happy; his laughter was filled with so much life and excitement. I placed my hand on my stomach and thought about my unborn fetus. It had been a week since I'd found out that I was pregnant, and I still hadn't told Big Daddy. I didn't know how to tell him, but I knew I had to tell him soon.

~ ~ ~

Whenever we had downtime, Jenny taught me different things about skin types. I loved working with her. She made sure I understood everything she taught me before we moved on to something else. Lately, my morning sickness had been getting the best of me. I lost five pounds in one week.

"Hey, Keisha." Jenny walked up behind me as I finished a phone call. Her eyes held a look of compassion. "I've decided that I don't need you here anymore. I love you being here, but I want you to take care of yourself."

My eyes filled with tears. "You're firing me?" I asked Jenny.

"No! Of course not. I've learned a lot from you, and you've kept me well organized." She patted me on the back. "I can handle everything here, but I would love to have you work from home, keeping me organized and keeping everything on schedule."

"Really?" I looked up at her, my eyes growing wider. "Of course, I will. I thought you were firing me." I wiped my teary eyes.

"No, I love you. You're like a little sister to me."

"Aw, I love you too," I replied to Jenny as we hugged.

On the drive home, I called Big Daddy and told him how I was now going to work from home and still receive the same pay and benefits. Of course, he was excited for me.

Later that night, Big Daddy greeted me at the door with a kiss on the lips.

"I have something for you," I said as we walked to my bedroom.

"You do?" Big Daddy asked with excitement, wrapping his arms around me from behind.

I grabbed a box from my closet. I'd even wrapped it in giftwrap earlier. I had taken yet another pregnancy test to confirm that I was surely pregnant—not to mention the five other pregnancy tests that I had taken previously. I started to feel nerves and anxious. I didn't know how Big daddy would react to the news.

"You actually got me something? What is it?"

"Well, open it." I stood in front of him, sweating like a contestant on American Idol just before the announcement of the winner.

"What's wrong, boo?" Big Daddy asked when tears started to fall from my eyes. "Talk to me, girl, what's up?"

"Just open it."

Big Daddy opened the box and took the pregnancy stick out that read "pregnant." He stared at it for what seemed to have been two minutes.

"Well, say something." I broke the silence.

"I don't know what to say, Keisha. How did this happen?" he asked calmly.

"Whatever." Disappointed with his reaction, I threw my hand up and walked away.

"Baby, look, I'm sorry." He followed and grabbed my hand. "It's just, I wasn't expecting this AT ALL." He took a deep breath.

"Neither was I, Hector. I don't know what to do." I cried. "I'm scared, confused, mad, angry, and I'm very, very emotional."

Big Daddy pulled me closer. "Keisha, I love you, girl. I'm scared too, but we're in this together. I PROMISE you that I will do what I have to do as a man to make sure you, Li'l T, and the baby have everything y'all need. I ain't like that sucka ass nigga T. My mom raised me right. She taught me to be a man and take care of my responsibilities."

I couldn't respond because my tears flowed like rivulets down my face.

"I love you, girl." Big Daddy held me tight. "Wonderful is you."

"Wonderful is we," I whispered, wiping my eyes.

"Together forever, the way it's gonna be. I love your touch, your kiss, I just love the way you make me feel, baby, I'm for real. You my boo today, tomorrow, and every day, and that's the way it will remain." We quoted *Wonderful* together in unison.

Congratulations

I had just finished washing the dishes, when my mom called. I stretched out on the couch and talked to her. It had been three weeks and we hadn't told anyone that we were pregnant, except for our moms. They both were excited for us. Big Daddy's mom was more excited because she was expecting her first grandchild.

~ ~ ~

I opened the front door to find Big Daddy standing there with a dozen red roses in his hand.

"Aw, baby, you are so sweet. You got me roses." I hugged him and kissed him on the lips.

"Yeah, girl, you deserve it. Tomorrow I'm going to take you out so that we can REALLY celebrate your pregnancy. Now give Big Daddy more of them lips."

I kissed his lips and our tongues tangled and danced together.

~ ~ ~

"Babe, wake up. I got plans for us this morning." Big Daddy kissed me on the forehead. "I made breakfast because we got a big day ahead of us. Now get up and go eat."

"Yes, sir!" I said sarcastically as I got up to shower.

After we ate, we dropped Li'l T off with my mom and headed out of the city.

"Where are we going, boo?" I asked Big Daddy.

"Just sit back and ride, girl. Do you trust me?" He glanced at me.

"You know I do, boo." I smiled.

"Alright then." Big Daddy grabbed my hand and kissed the back of it while he continued to drive.

An hour later, we arrived at a place called *Together,* tucked between a clothing store and a health food outlet in a contemporary shopping plaza.

"Wait here, girl. I will be right back." Big Daddy got out of the car.

"OK." *I wonder what he's up to.*

It took Big Daddy four minutes to return to the car. He opened the door for me and walked me into the place. As I walked in, a woman greeted and approached me.

"Hello, Ms. Keisha. How are you today?" asked the woman, a thin Caucasian dressed in all white with her hair pulled back into a tight ponytail.

"I'm blessed," I replied, wondering how she knew my name.

"Y'all be sure to take care of my girl," Big Daddy told her.

"What you mean, boo?" I asked confused.

"Babe, I gotta make a run real quick, but I'm going to be back soon. They're going to take care of you. I love you." He kissed me on the lips.

"I love you too."

"Don't worry, Mr. Marrero, we're going to take good care of Ms. Keisha," the woman replied to him.

Big Daddy walked out of the shop and the lady, who never told me her name, motioned for me to follow her. We entered a room that took me by surprise. The walls were painted purple and lime green, which were my two favorite colors. The large crystal-clear waterfall in the center of the room was breathtaking. The aroma in the room smelled so sweet, and the relaxing music made me wanna crawl into bed.

Two ladies stood in the doorway. They also wore all white and slick ponytails.

"Hello, Ms. Keisha. How are you?" said one of the two ladies.

"I'm blessed."

"My name is Ruth, and this is Naomi, and we're here to make you feel relaxed. We want you to forget all of your worries and all of your problems."

"OK."

"Mr. Marrero wanted you to have the whole package, so today you will be receiving a full body massage, a manicure, and a pedicure. Here's a robe for you." She handed me a plush white robe. "You can change into it and hit the call button when you're ready for us to come back in."

"OK." *I can't believe he did this. He's so sweet to me.*

I changed into the robe and hit the button. The ladies returned and gave me a massage from the top of my head to the soles of my feet. Ruth worked on my top half, and she made the tension in my neck disappear. Naomi worked on my bottom half and she hit all of my gait points. After two hours of being pampered, I was all done.

My body felt relaxed and free from any stress that I may have had. When I walked out of the room and into the waiting room, I saw Big daddy.

"Hey, babe, did you enjoy yourself?" Big Daddy wore black pants with a long-sleeved black dress shirt and a black and white vest over it.

"Yes. I did, boo." I smiled and took a breath of air. "You didn't have to do this for me. Do you have enough money for this?" I asked seriously when I noticed the price of the package.

"Baby, as long as you're happy, that's all that matters. When it comes to you, there is no limit on money, girl." He gazed into my eyes, making me feel like the most beautiful woman in the world.

"How did I get so lucky to have you?"

"Nah, girl, how did I get so lucky to have YOU." He kissed me on the lips.

"Baby, why did you change clothes? You didn't have this on earlier."

"No, I didn't, and you're going to change too. I got you something." Big Daddy walked to a chair and grabbed a black bag. He unzipped the bag and pulled out a beautiful black lace gown.

"Is that for me?" I asked with my mouth wide open.

"Of course it is, girl. Go put it on," he demanded.

Ruth and Naomi smiled as I stepped into the bathroom to change. It fit perfectly. My stomach wasn't showing yet, so the dress hugged my body, showing off my curves and making me feel like a super star.

"Damn, girl, you sexy as hell!"

"Thanks, boo, you sexy too."

"Well, I can't let you wear that dress without the shoes to go along with it." Big Daddy handed me a pair of black and gold heels.

"Bae, you are too good to me." I smiled. "Why are we dressing up?"

"Do you trust me, girl?" he asked.

"You know I do."

"A'ight then. You deserve every bit of it, girl!"

"Thank you, boo. I love you!"

"I love you more, girl!" He kissed my forehead.

~ ~ ~

Two hours later, we arrived at a brick building that stood alone. The entrance had glass doors, but they were dark, revealing nothing inside. I'd never seen this place before. There were no windows on the building, no cars around it, and the place looked deserted.

"What is this place?" I asked.

"You trust me, right?" Big Daddy pulled out his phone and sent a text to someone.

"Yes, baby, I do." I couldn't help but wonder what he was up to, but I also trusted him, and I trusted his judgement.

Whomever he texted must have texted him back because I heard his phone go off.

"OK, boo, let's go in."

He held open the door for me and I stepped into darkness. I wanted to trust Big Daddy's judgement, but my mind told me to turn back around and get in the car.

"OK, boo, what's going on here? Why is it so dark?" Goosebumps arose on my skin, and I reached for his hand.

"I'm not sure, boo, but come on." Big Daddy continued to walk, leading me down a hallway. He opened the next set of doors and told me to go in first.

As hesitant as I was, I followed his instructions and walked through the doorway ahead of him.

"SURPRISE! CONGRATULATIONS!" Yelled our families and some members from our church as the lights came on.

We stood in a gorgeous room, everything in black and gold, from the balloons to the decorations. It reminded me of when I went to the prom with a boy named Ray. Several tables held food; there was soul food and there was Spanish food. A cake decorated in gold and white and with my picture on it read "Congratulations, Keisha, we love you!"

I looked at Big Daddy and gave him a big hug. "What is all of this? What's the occasion?"

"You are the occasion, girl. You're my woman, and I wanted to celebrate you." He gazed into my eyes with passion.

"I love you so much, baby." As I held his gaze, I thought how lucky I was to have a man like him.

"I love you too, girl. Now you enjoy yourself."

Li'l T was the first person I went to. He looked so cute. He and Big Daddy wore matching outfits: black pants with a long-sleeved black dress shirt and a black and white vest over it. My men were so handsome, and I loved them so much. After eating and conversing with both families, Big Daddy led me to a chair to open the gifts. Almost everyone gave me gift cards for the baby.

Some got baby clothes and diapers, but I was anxious to open a big box in pastel wrap that sat on the end of the table.

"Babe, this one is from me." Big Daddy set the huge box in front of me.

"I wonder what it is. It's so big. Give me a hint." I smiled, hoping he'd give me a hint.

"Nah, girl, just open it." He winked at me.

I lifted the lid to find another well-wrapped box inside. A few people laughed and commented. I unwrapped that box to find another box inside it. More laughter and someone clapped. As I opened that box, I found another box wrapped up neatly. I tore the paper to find another box inside. Family members and friends laughed and commented again, everyone wondering how many boxes I'd go through to reach the actual gift. Was there an actual gift?

"OK, is this some kind of joke, Big Daddy?" I asked, getting upset.

"Just open it, girl," Big Daddy replied as he and the crowd laughed.

"This is not funny. Why would you wrap all these boxes? The boxes are getting smaller and smaller."

"Baby, just open them for me. Do you trust me?"

"You know I do." I unwrapped the paper to find another box, only this time this box had something in it.

Big Daddy took the box from my hand, stood in front of me and got down on one knee.

Tears formed in my eyes. *Is he about to do what I think he's about to do?* I asked myself.

"Keisha, you know I love you, and you know I love Li'l T as if he was my own son. From the very first time I saw you, I knew you were down to ride, and I knew I had to make you mine. I love your family and I would love to make you a part of my family, now that we've started our own family. Keisha"—he paused—"I would love to make you my wife. Will you marry me?" He stared into my eyes.

I never thought the day would come that Big Daddy would ask me to marry him, and now that it was finally here, I was in shock. I loved him deeply. Words couldn't explain the love I had for this man. There was only one answer I could give.

"Yes! Yes, baby, yes, I would love to marry you," I replied as the tears ran down my face. Big Daddy and I kissed and hugged as everyone cheered and congratulated us.

"Wonderful is you," he whispered.

"Wonderful is we," I whispered back.

"Together forever, the way it's gonna be. I love your touch, your kiss, I just love the way you make me feel, baby, I'm for real. You my boo today, tomorrow, and every day, and that's the way it will remain." We quoted *Wonderful* together in unison.

Tragedy

I put Li'l T down for a nap and went to my bedroom to lie down. It had been almost a month since Big Daddy proposed to me; I was so in love with him. He made me feel so special in ways I'd never imagined.

"What's up, girl?" Big Daddy walked into my room and turned off the TV.

"What's up, babe?" I replied.

"What day did you schedule the first appointment?" He sat on the bed and rubbed my arm.

"Next month on the 28th." I smiled. "I can't wait to find out if we're having a girl or a boy."

"Neither can I, boo."

"Do you want a girl or a boy?" I asked.

"As long as I have a healthy baby, that's all that matters to me, girl."

"How did I get so lucky to have you?" I asked.

Without responding Big Daddy got down on his knees.

"What are you doing, babe. I already said yes that I will marry you."

Big Daddy grabbed my hand and looked me in my eyes.

"Keisha, I love you so much! You changed me for the better. Because of you, I don't smoke weed anymore, I don't cuss *as much* anymore, and most of all I have a relationship with God. I love you for that, girl. Being with you has given me a different outlook on life itself. I just wanna do right by you as well as our unborn child. I love you, girl."

"Aw, baby, I love you so much!" I became full of emotion.

~ ~ ~

Later that day, Big Daddy and I went out on a date to enjoy each other. We had a great time together as we went to dinner and out dancing. I loved spending time with him. We returned to the house around midnight. As I was getting ready for bed, my stomach started to cramp terribly. When I went to the bathroom, I noticed some spotting. When I was pregnant with Li'l T, I never bled or had cramps, to my knowledge.

Big Daddy appeared in the bathroom doorway. "Hey, what's wrong? Do you want to go to the ER?"

"No." I shook my head. "I'm just gonna take a nice warm shower and lie down."

"OK, boo. I love you."

"I love you too." Holding my tummy, I headed for the shower.

The next morning, I woke up in excruciating pain. I didn't get much sleep during the night because of the intensity of the cramps. When I went to the bathroom, I noticed blood clots. My first thoughts went to the baby.

"Babe," I shouted, "take me to the Emergency Room."

At the ER, they took an ultrasound and took my blood. After five hours of waiting for the results, the doctor knocked on the door of my examination room.

"Hello, I'm Doctor Nupe. How are y'all doing?"

"Hi. Is everything OK with the baby?" I asked, concerned.

The doctor gave me a sad sort of smile and took a step closer. "I'm sorry to say, but it looks like you had what we call a threatening miscarriage. Your human chorionic gonadotropin, which we call HCG, levels are really low, and the ultrasound didn't show much of anything. I believe you passed the baby on your own, so we don't have to do a DNC on you. I wish I had better news for you." The doctor spoke nonchalantly.

In that moment, I became numb. I didn't know what the doctor was talking about, but I'm sure he must've been confused. I looked at Big Daddy and he looked at me. There was a silence in the room.

"So, I lost the baby?" I finally spoke.

"Yes, I'm afraid so. I'll write you a prescription for the pain, but you will want to follow up with your doctor in a couple of days. It's important to get your blood drawn again in the next three days so your doctor can make sure your HCG levels continue to go down." Doctor Nupe spoke sternly. "Is there anything else I can do for you, Ms. O'Neil?" the doctor asked.

"No, thank you," I said as tears formed in my eyes.

"I will get the nurse so that she can write up your discharge papers."

~ ~ ~

We drove home in silence, neither Big Daddy nor I saying one word to the other. I cried silently to myself and wondered what I had done wrong for this to be happening. When I got home, Big Daddy made sure I was settled into bed, and then he went out to get my prescription from the drug store. I took a nap, and when I woke up Big Daddy wasn't back yet. I looked at the clock. He'd left three hours ago. I dialed his phone number but there was no answer. I called him again and again, and he still didn't answer.

Two hours later, after I'd called him multiple times, thinking the worst thoughts in my head, Big Daddy came stumbling into the bedroom.

"Are you drunk?" I asked him.

"Nah, girl. I just got a buzz going on." The smell of liquor filled the room.

"You don't even drink, Hector! Come on and lie down. You need to sleep that off!" I demanded.

"I love you," Big Daddy said.

"I love you too, but this is a no-no. This isn't you! What if Li'l T was here and seen you like this? You know what? Just get some rest. We will talk in the morning." I covered him up and lay next to him, facing the opposite direction. *I can't believe he's drunk. I lose a baby, and this is what he does?*

The next morning, I woke up to breakfast in bed. I didn't have an appetite, but I forced myself to eat something. My emotions were all over the place, and Big Daddy hadn't made it any better coming to the house drunk. After taking a few bites, I rested my head on my pillow.

"Keisha." Big Daddy sat on the edge of the bed and grabbed my hand. "Look, baby, I'm sorry about last night. I don't know what came over me. I wanted to talk about what happened when we found out the news, but I didn't want to overwhelm you. I went to the store to get your prescription, and I got a call from Felipe. It was his birthday and he wanted me to come out with him and the fellas. I don't even remember coming back here. But what I do remember is waking up to you and realizing that I don't ever wanna lose you over some dumb shit that I had done. I love you, girl."

"I love you too, and thank God you made it here safe." I turned over to go back to sleep.

~ ~ ~

It had been three days since I'd found out about the miscarriage. I'd been getting irritated at the smallest things, and Big Daddy was becoming annoying to me. Every five minutes or so he would ask me if I was OK.

"I'm sorry, babe. I just want to make sure my girl is OK," Big Daddy said.

"I'm fine. I just need to get out of this house! I've been in here for three whole days. Can you keep an eye on Li'l T? I'm gonna go for a drive," I spat as I grabbed my jacket and fiddled for my keys.

"Of course, baby. Do you need me to drive you anywhere?" Big Daddy compassionately asked.

"No! Never mind. I'll take Li'l T and go to my mom's for a while." I got my purse, picked up Li'l T, and walked out the door.

On the drive to my mom's, I sobbed like a baby. What had I done wrong for me to lose the baby? The pain that I felt was unreal. It all seemed like a bad dream that I couldn't wake up from.

The blast of a car horn interrupted my thoughts. I looked in the rearview mirror and saw a police car. Then I realized the traffic light had now turned green. I turned on my blinker and turned right so that I could collect my thoughts, then I noticed the cop car following me with the lights on. Sweating bullets, I stopped the car and placed both of my hands on the steering wheel. My heart sped up with each passing second.

After two minutes, the officer got out of his car, knocked on my window, and motioned for me to roll it down.

"I'm going to roll my window down now," I yelled through the glass while keeping my right hand visible on the steering wheel. I did this because I didn't want the officer drawing out his weapon on me.

"Ma'am, do you know why I pulled you over?" asked the officer.

"Because I was stopped at the green light?" I asked, shrugging my shoulders.

"I pulled you over because your taillight is out, and yes I did notice that you were at the light for a while. Is everything OK?" the officer asked with obvious concern.

"Honestly, officer, the other day I received some horrible news, and my mind must've been dwelling on it."

"I'm sorry to hear that. Do you have your license and registration, ma'am?"

"Yes, I do. It's in my purse. Is it OK if I reach in my purse for them?" I asked the officer. I was sure to tell him my every move because I didn't want to be the next Sandra Bland.

"Yes, go ahead." He waited patiently.

After handing him my license and registration, he went back to his car. Tears formed in my eyes again, but this time it was because I was terrified of the police, and I had my son in the car with me. I pulled out my cell phone and went live so that if anything were to happen to me it would be on video. It was a shame I felt it necessary to do this, but in today's world a person had to be careful. It seemed like we as African Americans were still fighting for our rights and fighting for our lives. It was as if the world didn't see us as equals even today.

Almost every time I turned on the news, I heard about a police officer killing yet another black person. I thought they were supposed to serve and protect us. True, there were good cops out there, but the bad cops made all of them look bad across America. I couldn't imagine how the mother of young Tamir Elijah Rice felt when she'd discovered that her baby had been shot and killed by a cop. As a mother, hearing about things like that made me sad and feel sympathy—even though it wasn't my child.

I thought how that could've been my child, especially since I was raising a son. Not just any son but raising a black son in today's world.

"Mommy, are you OK?" Li'l T asked, interrupting my thoughts.

"Yes, baby, mommy is fine. I just have something in my eyes," I lied as I grabbed a napkin from the glovebox and wiped my eyes.

"Why you didn't get it out yet? Do you want me to blow it for you?"

"No, baby, I will get it. Thank you for offering though." I looked back and smiled at my baby.

"You're welcome, Mommy. I love you!"

"I love you too, baby." I couldn't help but to cry more. Li'l T was a very sweet young man, and I couldn't imagine my life without him.

"Ma'am." The officer came back to the car, interrupting my thoughts again. "I see that you have a clean record, so I'm going to let you go with a warning. I want you to get your taillight fixed as soon as possible." He smiled and handed me my license.

"OK, thank you, officer," I said wiping my tears.

"Not all of us are bad cops," he said, as if reading my mind. "Enjoy the rest of your day, ma'am." He smiled and walked away.

I was grateful that I didn't get a ticket, but most of all I was thankful for my life.

Valentine's Day

I was lying in bed as I often did lately. It had been two weeks since the miscarriage and neither Big Daddy nor I had talked about it. Deep down my heart was hurting. I didn't know how to tell him because he's a man, and I thought he wouldn't understand what I was going through. Big Daddy and I never argued about anything in the past before, but now we started to argue about the smallest things: why he left the cap off the toothpaste, or why he had to chew so loudly. I tried to go on with my daily life, but inside I felt empty. I felt lost. I felt like less of a woman because I'd been unable to carry the baby to full term.

There must be something wrong with me, I said to myself. I didn't carry Li'l T full term, so it had to have been me. Big Daddy had been so excited to learn that I was pregnant, and now I couldn't even give him a baby. *What's wrong with me?*

"Hey, baby, do you need anything?" Big Daddy peeked his head into the bedroom.

"No," I spat rudely, feeling sorry for myself.

"You didn't have to get smart, Keisha. I was just trying to be nice." He stepped into the bedroom.

I rolled away from him and didn't reply.

"I'm gonna go to my mom's crib. I'm gonna give you some time to cool down."

"Whatever. I don't need time to cool down!"

"Keisha, you have a problem with EVERYTHING I do." Big Daddy raised his voice and moved closer to the bed. "I'm chewing too loudly. I didn't put the toilet seat down. Lately, nothing I do is right to you. I'm this, I'm that. I'm tired of going back and forth with you, girl. You know I don't even get down like that, so either we talk about it, or we let it go."

I rolled over to face him and shoot him an accusing glare. "Let it go! So it's that easy to let it go, huh, Hector?" I spoke as tears welled in my eyes.

"It was my baby too, Keisha!" he yelled, slapping a hand to his chest. "You're not the only one going through it! Do you think it's easy for me to act like nothing ever happened? It's hard on me too, girl. I suffered a loss as well as you did. No, it wasn't my body, but it was my baby! I have to walk around here like I'm strong, but deep down I'm struggling like a muthafucka. It's hard for me, especially when you keep shutting me out and acting like everything I do is so wrong." Tears formed in Big Daddy's eyes.

I pushed myself up on my elbows, regret creeping in. I'd never seen Big Daddy cry before. I felt awful. Here I was lost in my feelings over the miscarriage and not thinking about what it had done to him. He'd been helping take care of Li'l T this entire time while I moped around feeling sorry for myself. He must've thought I was an awful person.

"Baby, I'm sorry." I sat up in bed and wrapped my arms around my waist. "I didn't know you felt that way."

"You never asked how I felt either." His voice softened. "I ask how you're feeling daily, and mainly because I don't want you to feel the way I do. I'm the man, which means I'm supposed to be the strong one. But now all I want is some respect, Keisha. Lately, you've been speaking to me in a way that you've never spoken to me before, and that hurts me too. I feel like you don't give a fuck about nothing anymore. I've been taking care of Li'l T by myself for two weeks, while you lay in bed feeling sorry for yourself. I know it's tough, but we can try again. God will never put more on us than we can bear."

"You're right, baby. I'm so sorry." My tears formed a small spot on my t-shirt. "I'll try to do better, and I thank you for being here, and I thank you for looking after Li'l T. You are such an amazing man." I cried as I got up from the bed and hugged him.

"You're an amazing woman. Nah, girl, you're wonderful." He hugged me back.

"Wonderful is you, wonderful is we, together forever, the way it's gonna be. I love your touch, your kiss, I just love the way you make me feel, baby, I'm for real. You my boo today, tomorrow, and every day, and that's the way it will remain." We quoted *Wonderful* together in unison.

~ ~ ~

A week had passed, and I slowly began to feel normal again. Big Daddy and I were doing better. It was almost Valentine's Day and I didn't know what I was going to get him. I wanted to do something extra special to show him how much he meant to me. If I could give Big Daddy the world, I would. I wasn't sure if he wanted to get me anything because of the way I'd been acting towards him.

~ ~ ~

Today was Valentine's Day, and while Big Daddy was at work, I sent Li'l T with my mom so that Big Daddy and I would have the house to ourselves. I cleaned the house from top to bottom, while the scent of warm vanilla candles burned throughout the house and up the stairs. Close to the time Big Daddy would get home from work, I hopped into the shower. The smell of Britney Spears' "Fantasy" filled the room as I lotioned my body. I slipped into my pink lingerie with the matching boy shorts that I had bought specifically for this day.

As I went back downstairs, I received a text from Big Daddy. *I'm outside.*

Before I opened the door, I made sure everything was in its proper place. I opened the door to find Big Daddy standing there looking sexier than ever. His hair was freshly cut and perfectly lined up, and he looked more handsome than ever.

"Damn, girl, you are so sexy!" Big Daddy said as he hugged and kissed me.

"I thought you already knew that," I said with a smile.

"I did. That's why you will be the future Mrs. Marrero."

"I love the sound of that, Mr. Marrero." I led him up the stairs and into the candlelit bedroom. I'd strewn candy hearts that read "I love you" across the bed. "I love you, Big Daddy, and I never want to lose you. I apologize for my words and actions," I said as a tear rolled down my face.

"Bae, you know I forgive you, but did you really have to start crying now? A nigga thought he was about to get some." He laughed.

"I'm sorry. I just wanted you to know how sorry I am. I know it's been rough on you too, and I just want to move past this together and grow from this experience."

"We will, babe, don't worry." Big Daddy kissed my forehead. "I'll be back. I'm going to run to the car right quick."

"Uh . . . OK."

He returned with a huge bear in his arms. The bear's pink shirt read "I Love You" in red letters. And he also brought in a box of chocolate Reese's.

"Aw, babe, thank you! I love it." I smiled and hugged the plush bear.

"I wanted to surprise you later on, but I couldn't resist—especially after seeing you tear up. I thought it might bring a smile to your face."

"Well, it worked." I continued to hug the bear and smile. "Well, since you're giving gifts, go and look in your top drawer."

Big Daddy did what he was told. When he returned, he was smiling uncontrollably and holding the watch and outfit that I had gotten for him.

"This me?" Big Daddy replied excitedly.

"Yes, baby."

Big Daddy took me into his arms and kissed me passionately. We made our way to the bed, but things didn't go any further than kissing.

"I can't do this, babe. I'm sorry." I pulled away. "I thought I was going to be able to, but I just feel like it's too soon, and I don't want to rush anything or take any chances."

"Do you want me to get some condoms?" He looked disappointed.

"No, can you just hold me?"

Big Daddy did as he was told. "I got you, babe." Big Daddy held me.

I lay on his chest and cried like a baby. All I could think about was the miscarriage and how I was unable to carry the child to full term.

Better

After finishing up a call with a patient, I logged off my computer for the day. It'd been a month, and I'd been trying to get back to myself with work and taking care of Li'l T. Big Daddy and I were getting better as each day passed.

"Hey, baby." I answered the phone on the third ring.

"What's up, girl? Open the door," Big Daddy replied on the other end.

"OK." I went downstairs and unlocked the door for Big Daddy. When he entered, we greeted each other with a kiss on the lips.

"Did you miss me?" I asked Big Daddy.

"You know I did, girl. Did you miss me?"

"Of course, I did, boo. I've wanted to kiss your lips all day." I gave him another kiss on the lips.

"I've missed you so much, girl, that I got these for you." Big Daddy brought a bouquet of red roses from behind his back.

"Aw, baby, they're beautiful. Thank you." I kissed his lips once again. Then I grabbed his hand and led him upstairs. For the first time in months, our souls collaborated together.

"Wonderful is you," I whispered as I rested on Big Daddy's chest.

"Wonderful is we," he whispered back.

"Together forever, the way it's gonna be. I love your touch, your kiss, I just love the way you make me feel, baby, I'm for real. You my boo today, tomorrow, and every day, and that's the way it will remain." We quoted *Wonderful* together in unison as we cuddled up and fell asleep.

~ ~ ~

"Get dressed, girl, and wear something nice. I made reservations for us," Big Daddy told me the day after our wonderful night together.

"Where are we going?" I asked.

"Do you trust me, girl?" Big Daddy looked at me with his sexy brown eyes.

"Of course, I do," I said with a bashful smile.

"A'ight, then just do what I say." He winked at me.

"OK, Mr. Marrero."

Two hours later, we both were dressed and ready to go. He drove to a nice restaurant in the next town over called *The Brazo*. We pulled in front of the restaurant and let the valet park our car for us. Big Daddy held the door open for me. The high decorated ceilings with dark ambient lighting made the place beautiful inside.

An all-you-can-eat salad bar stood in the middle of the restaurant. Waiters came to the tables, offering a variety of meats.

"Babe, this place is nice." I held onto his arm.

"Yeah, Felipe told me about this spot. I've never been, and of course I wanted to take the future Mrs. Marrero." He gave me a sweet glance and kissed my forehead.

"You are so good to me, Big Daddy." I smiled as we walked to our table.

"Hi, my name is Jessie, and I will be your server today. Can I offer you a cocktail or bottle of champagne?"

"Um." I searched the menu to find the drinks. "I'll just have a water." I looked up at our server and noticed she was pregnant. Thoughts of my unborn baby ran through my mind.

"OK, and how about you, sir?"

"I'll have the same."

"How many months are you?" I asked Jessie.

"I'm seven months." She rubbed her belly and smiled.

"Cool," I managed to say with a slight smile.

"I'll be right back with your drinks, and you are welcome to the salad bar."

"Hey, babe, I'm gonna run to the bathroom real fast." I told Big Daddy.

"OK, boo, hurry back."

I walked into the bathroom, my breathing becoming heavier, and I began to sweat uncontrollably. Splashing water on my neck, I tried to pull myself together. I didn't want Big Daddy to see me like this. The attacks had started about a month ago, but I hid them from Big Daddy. I didn't want him to find out that I was still bitter about the miscarriage, and now it was to the point that I would have a panic attack whenever something reminded me of me being pregnant.

"Keisha, are you OK?" an unfamiliar voice spoke. "Mr. Marrero asked me to check on you."

That's when I realized it was Jessie's voice that I heard. "Tell him I'll be out in a second. I'm just not feeling well."

"OK."

Pull it together, Keisha, pull it together, I told myself as I splashed my face with cold water.

A few minutes later, someone knocked on the girl's restroom door. "Hey, babe, you OK in there?" Big Daddy said.

"I'm fine, babe," I lied.

"Nah, you don't sound fine. I'm coming in." The door swung open and Big Daddy walked into the women's bathroom. "What's wrong, babe?" He gave me a sympathetic look.

"I don't know." Tears welled in my eyes and my emotions let loose. "Can we go home?" I said between sobs. I was grateful that Big Daddy didn't question my reason to leave, instead he just did what he was asked.

We drove home in silence. When we got home, Big Daddy drew me a warm bath.

"I made the bed and laid out a pair of pajamas for you. I'll sleep on the couch, but let me know if you need anything." Big Daddy kissed my forehead and walked out of the bathroom.

Thankful as I was for his kindness, I couldn't reply to him. I could only cry. I didn't even know what I was crying about, but the tears wouldn't stop streaming down my face. I felt sad and alone, but I wasn't alone. I had Big Daddy, even though I didn't want him here. I wanted to be alone. Once I seemed to have run out of tears, I wiped my face and realized that my bath was now cold and my entire body wrinkled. Reaching for my towel, I got out of the tub and passed out on the bed without dressing in my pajamas.

~ ~ ~

"Good morning, babe. How are you feeling?" Big Daddy asked. Then I felt his lips on my forehead.

"I'm better, thank you." I pulled the blanket over my chin as I lay in bed.

"I made breakfast. I didn't know if I should bring it to you or not, but I made it for whenever you're ready to eat." He grabbed my hand.

"I appreciate it, babe, and I thank you for being here with me and for me. I don't deserve you." I felt sort of empty.

"Keisha, you are going to be my wife. There is absolutely nothing I wouldn't do for you." He gazed into my eyes, reassuring me that he wasn't going anywhere.

"I've been thinking." I started to cry.

"You know what? I've been thinking too, girl. We haven't prayed together about the situation. I think we should do that. I know it will make you feel better." He dropped down to his knees and looked to the Lord.

"That's not what I was thinking," I rudely replied, though it touched me to see his faith. My faith was faltering.

"Keisha, baby, when I first met you, you were on fire for God. Since the miscarriage happened, you haven't been going to church like you used to. You used to be at church all the time throughout the week, but now we only go on Sunday's and sometimes you don't even want to go then." He paused. "I'm your man, and it's my job to push you and make you better, so that's what I'm gonna do."

"I don't feel like praying right now, babe. Could you go to your mom's house? I just want to be alone." It pained me to say that to my future husband, but I wanted to be alone. I was tired of everything and everyone, and my emotions had spun out of control.

"Really? Is that how you feel, Keisha? Is it because I wanted to pray?" Big Daddy asked with a confused look on his face.

"No, it's because I'm sick and tired of you! I'm tired of you always being nice to Li'l T. I'm tired of you always thinking about me and trying to take care of me! What's wrong with you?" I shouted. Anger began to creep in, and I didn't understand why.

"You're not making any sense, girl!" He stood up. "I'm gonna go to my mom's house and let you cool down. I'm not sure where all of this is coming from, Keisha, but I was just trying to do what any real man would do and take care of his woman!"

"Whatever." I waved my hand at him.

"I think you should talk to someone. Since you lost the baby, you haven't been yourself. You lash out for no reason, you have emotional breakdowns, and you haven't seen Li'l T in three days. We were supposed to take him to the park today, or did you forget?"

"Don't you ever say anything about MY son! And who the fuck do *I* need to talk to, huh? So now you think I'm crazy? Is that what it is? You know what? GET OUT! I don't need you. In fact, I don't need this ring either," I shouted as I took off my engagement ring and threw it at his face.

"That was foul, girl, and you know it." Big Daddy did not respond with anger. "Keisha, baby, don't do this." He walked over to me with open arms. "Remember we told each other that no matter how mad we get at one another, you would NEVER take off the ring, and I would NEVER ask for it back."

"Fuck you!" I shouted as I pushed his hands away from me.

"Wow! I hope you get the help you need, Keshia. I love you, but I can't do this. I tried and tried to help you through, but I'm not gonna keep letting you disrespect me as if I'm nothing." Big Daddy cried as he walked out of the door.

My emotions swarmed through my mind and escaped with a gut-wrenching scream. I covered my ears, not wanting to hear the ugly sound coming out of me, but I didn't stop screaming. The pain didn't lessen. It wouldn't go away, so I flung myself from my bed and swiped the framed pictures from my night table.

Insanity

I lay in bed as I often did, thinking about Big Daddy, but I thought about my unborn child more. Two weeks passed since Big Daddy and I ended things. I lied and told my mom that Big Daddy and I were going on a trip and we couldn't have cell phones. I didn't want her to worry about me when she couldn't get in touch with me. I turned my cell phone off and shut myself out from the world. I felt so lost. I barely ate and had lost ten pounds.

I finally built up enough strength to clean up the broken glass and picture frames that I'd broken when Big Daddy left. I couldn't stay in the place that I was in. I didn't want to pray, so I called my mom to tell her what had happened and how I was feeling now. Of course, she wanted to pray with me, but I didn't want to. I was upset with God. I couldn't believe He let this happen to me, and He knew it would cause me so much pain.

Later that day, my mom came to check on me, but I didn't feel like being bothered so I didn't open the door. The front door opened anyway, jogging my memory: I'd given her a key when I first moved in.

"Ra' Keisha, Ra' Keisha!" my mom yelled. "Are you here?" She made her way up the stairs and found me lying in the bed. "Girl, what is wrong with you? You ain't been answering the phone. Can't no one get ahold of you. I know you're sad but, baby girl, you have to pull it together. Women are strong. We get knocked down, but we always get back up."

"I don't feel strong." I used my sheet to wipe away my tears.

"Your son misses you, Keisha."

"I know." I turned and looked at Li'l T's picture on my nightstand. "I miss him so much. I just don't want him to see me like this. I need to be strong when he comes home. I can't let him see me like this. I'm a mess."

"Well, get up!" my mom ordered. "Get in the shower and we'll go see him."

"I can't." I pulled the covers over my head and rolled away from her.

"Well, what are you gonna do? I'm not leaving you here like this. I think you need to talk to somebody, Keisha."

"Now you sound like Big Daddy."

"Well, he loves you, and so do I. But I'm not gonna leave just because you tell me to."

"Oh my God, Mom!" I yelled into the pillow.

"Girl, I don't care about you getting mad! Get up and take a shower. You're too pretty to smell like that."

Instead of snapping at her, I did what I was told and got in the shower. After my shower, I packed some clothes so that I could stay at my mom's house for a couple of days. After an hour of being at my mom's house and seeing Li'l T, I wanted to go back home and lie in my bed.

"Hey, mom, I'll be back. I forgot something at home." I got up from the couch faking a smile so she wouldn't suspect.

"You need me to go with you?" she asked, setting her book aside.

"No, I'll be right back." I walked backwards, looking at her while fumbling through my purse for my keys.

"You make sure you come RIGHT back," she ordered, narrowing her eyes.

"OK."

Twenty minutes later, I found myself sitting in front of the hospital, debating whether or not I should go inside. I was a complete mess, and I wasn't able to take care of my son. When he saw me walk through the front door at my mom's house, his face lit up so brightly and he ran and hugged me so tightly. When I felt his arms, a bit of peace ran through my body, but it wasn't enough to keep me sane.

I shut off the engine of my car and opened the door. I'd built up enough courage to walk through the hospital doors and check myself in. After getting registered, they gave me a pink slip and wheeled me up to the psych ward.

~ ~ ~

I called my mom to let her know that I had checked myself into the hospital and to get help with Li'l T. She told me that I should have called Bishop Bernard, but I told her that if I wanted the help, I had to get it on my own and get it my way and some preacher wasn't gonna change the way I felt.

Three days later, I didn't feel any different. Doctors and counselors came in and tried talking to me, but I politely declined their offers. *I should have never come here and checked myself in. These people in here are crazy, and I'm not nearly as bad as some people are,* I told myself.

I'd met people in here that wanted to kill themselves, and people that just wanted a place to sleep, and I also met people who had nothing wrong with them. If they wanted to keep their social security benefits, they had to check in somewhere and talk to someone.

"Ra' Keisha, you have a visitor," Nurse Becky said as she came into my room.

"Tell my mom that she doesn't have to come see me every day." I rolled my eyes.

"It's not your mom," she replied.

Who else could it be? No one knows I'm in here. I got up and went to the waiting room and peeked through the double doors so that I could see who'd come to see me. Big Daddy stood there in a white t-shirt and jeans, looking sexier than ever. I missed him so much. I wanted to jump into his arms and never let go. But I couldn't let him see me like this. I'd treated him like crap, and I felt awful about it.

"Tell him that I can't have any visitors," I told Becky.

I watched him walk away, tears forming in my eyes. As I returned to my room, a patient stopped me.

"Ra' Keisha is your name, right?" she asked.

"Yes."

"That's pretty. My name is Charlotte Hathaway." She extended her hand. Charlotte was a thin black woman that looked to be in her late fifties. She was very dark skinned with brown eyes. Something about her made me think she practiced voodoo, so I was a bit afraid of her, but *what's the harm in talking,* I thought.

"Hi." I shook her hand.

"Is this your first time in here?" she put her hand on my shoulder.

"Yes."

"I can tell. Would you like to come sit with me?"

Why would I wanna come sit with you, old woman? I asked myself underneath my breath. But I shocked myself with the answer that I gave her.

"Sure."

She fixed herself a cup of coffee and we sat down in silence.

"Why are you in here?" I asked Ms. Hathaway.

"Oh, chile, it seems like I come here every year around this time. You see, tomorrow is my son's birthday, but he's no longer here with me. He was shot and killed by the police because they thought he was someone else. My husband died of a heart attack ten years ago, so it's just me. I come here to talk to the counselors because my insurance doesn't cover counseling, but if I come here it's free." She smiled.

"I'm sorry."

"It's OK. The good Lord strengthens me every day, and I thank Him. He's the only thing keeping me in my right mind."

I felt at ease knowing Ms. Hathaway was a Christian. I found myself pouring my heart out to her.

"Are you alright, baby?" Ms. Hathaway asked.

"I had a miscarriage, and I can't seem to get over it," I said through fresh tears. "I questioned why God allowed this to happen to me."

"Chile, you sound like me." She smiled. "Not only did I question God, but I lost my faith. I asked God why He allowed my baby boy to get killed, and why He allowed the officers that shot him to get away with it and not show any compassion."

"Wow, so nothing happened to the officers?" I asked, concerned.

"Nope." She shook her head. "I spent weeks by my lonesome just feeling sorry for myself. I didn't have any family left. I decided I was going to take my own life." Her eyes started to water, and she put her head down. "I just wanted to get rid of all the emotional pain that I was feeling inside." She patted her face with a napkin.

"Well, on the day that I was gonna take my life, I sat and pondered on different ways that I could do it. I wanted it to be quick and painless. As I was walking down the street, a woman started talking to me. I didn't know the woman, never seen her a day in my life, but when we talked, I felt relieved." She looked up and smiled. "Just her presence made me feel better. She asked if I wanted to go to church with her because that's where she was headed. I didn't want to, but I did anyway. And I tell you I felt the presence of the Lord as soon as I walked in those church doors." She lifted her hands. "By the time church was over, I had forgotten about everything that was on my mind earlier that day, but I was at peace. You see, God sent that woman to talk to me, just like He's sending me to talk to you." Ms. Hathaway patted my hand.

Strange emotions overcame me—sadness, thankfulness, peace—and I just bowed my head and cried.

"I'm sorry about the miscarriage, and I know you're not going to get over it in one night. It might take days, weeks, even months, but you have to continue living life, baby girl. You can't let it pass you by, and you can't go on feeling sorry for yourself." She wiped my tears with a tissue. "Do you have other children?"

"Yes, ma'am, I have a son." I smiled as I thought about him.

"Well, baby, you have to get it together and be strong for him. Have you talked to any of the counselors yet?"

"No."

"Well, they're great. I think you should talk to them. There's no judgement or anything, just talking."

"Thank you!" I said to Ms. Hathaway.

"Your welcome, baby, and remember God will never put more on you than you can bear."

"I know. Will you pray for me?" I asked Ms. Hathaway to turn to God on my behalf.

"Of course I will, baby."

"Thanks again." I gave Ms. Hathaway a hug and went to my room.

~ ~ ~

I decided to take Ms. Hathaway's advice and speak with a counselor. After twelve days in the psych ward and finally talking with counselors, I was now able to be released. I felt better than when I first went in. They listened to my thoughts, my emotions, my fears and everything else that I shared. They gave me different techniques to use if I felt myself starting to get in a depressed place. They also suggested that I do grief counseling for a few weeks, but in order to do that, I had to remain at their facility.

That also meant more time away from Li'l T. I missed him so much already. But if I wanted to be the best me I could be, I had to make that choice, so I decided to go to grief counseling.

Big Daddy's View

Hector

As we waited in the crowded emergency room, I paced back and forth not knowing how I could comfort my future wife. The look on her face told me that she was just as nervous as I was. We'd been waiting here at the ER for five hours, and the doctor hadn't come in yet. I hoped everything was OK with the baby. I hoped it wasn't my fault.

I just wanted to go out and have a good time with my woman. Had that been too much on her body? It was rough seeing my future wife in so much pain. I wished I could do something to make it better for her. I loved this woman so much. She was the first girlfriend that I'd ever had, and she would be my last.

I was so grateful for her. I'd never thought I would want a family until I met her. And her son, Li'l T, was such an amazing kid. I would do anything for that li'l boy. I loved him like he was my own son. I loved him as much as I loved his mother. Now I was about to be a father to a child that I helped create. It just brought me so much joy.

We still had several months before the baby would come, but I couldn't wait until my li'l man was born. I was going to give him the world. I would be a great father. I wouldn't be like my daddy, or Andy's punk ass, and I definitely wouldn't be like that bitch ass nigga T.

A knock sounded on the door just before it opened. "Hello, I'm Doctor Nupe. How are y'all doing?" A short, middle-aged Indian man in a long white coat interrupted my thoughts.

"Hi. Is everything OK with the baby?" Keisha asked the question I wanted to know.

Using big words that made no sense to me, the doctor shattered my world. The baby had passed in a miscarriage. He didn't even know if it was a boy or a girl. We'd never know. Our child was gone.

On the drive home, neither of us said a word to the other. All that I could think about was how in just one hour I went from being so happy about being a father to discovering that I wouldn't be a father at all.

As devastated as I felt, I had to be strong for Keisha right now. She'd been sobbing to herself the entire time. I wasn't sure what to say to her, but maybe she wasn't ready to talk. I'd wait. She could talk when she felt ready.

After dropping her off at home, I went to pick up her prescription, but the tears streaming down my face made it hard to see. I pulled over to pull myself together. I couldn't let Keisha see me like this.

As I sat wiping my face with my shirt, my phone rang.

"What's up, my nigga?" I answered as if I hadn't been crying.

"What's good, homie? Yo', me and a couple of the fellas going down to Pauly's to have a drink or two for my birthday, and don't tell me you got other plans. Yo' fine ass future wife got you out here all sprung and shit, you can't even kick it with yo' best friend," Felipe said on the other end of the phone. Felipe and I had met in junior high school, over eight years ago. We shared the same classes together, and he's been my homeboy since then.

I forced a laugh. "Whatever, nigga, but I was actually on my way back to the house. I had to run to the store for her."

"See what I mean? I ain't seen you since the day you proposed to her. When is the next time I'll see you, on your wedding day?"

"Damn, has it been that long?"

"Bro!"

"I just found out some crazy shit too." I rubbed my head. "My mind all fucked up about it. I could use a drink."

"You good, bro? You know I got you if you ever need anything. You've been my best friend for years."

"Yeah, I know thanks, bro."

"So, you coming, right?" Felipe asked.

"Yeah, I'll meet y'all up there," I replied before I hung up.

A few minutes later, I pulled into the half-empty parking lot of Pauly's, a little dive on the edge of town that my friends and I loved. I walked in and spotted the fellas. They were easy to find because wherever Felipe was, a bunch of women were too, tailing around him. He was a lady's man.

"What's up, y'all?" I walked up to the VIP table that they stood around.

The fellas cheered and called out my name, as if it were my birthday. I shook hands with each of them and one offered me a shot of vodka.

"What's good, fam?" Felipe asked as he hugged my neck.

"Bro." My eyes watered as my thoughts returned to the baby we'd just lost.

Felipe's smile faded. "Let's step outside for a minute." He led me out the side door. "What's up, bro? Talk to me. You good?"

"Keisha, she . . . she had a miscarriage!" I broke down.

"Damn." Felipe wrapped his arm around my neck, comforting me as I sobbed. "Look, let's go inside and get a drink and forget about how fucked up life can be sometimes."

"Fuck it, let's turn up!" I wiped my tears.

I walked in ready to party. It was my best friend's birthday, and I was gonna celebrate with him. By the third shot, I was lit, but it seemed like shots just kept coming and coming, so I kept drinking them. When I finally thought to look at the time, it was almost midnight. I pulled out my phone and noticed a couple missed calls from Keisha, but I didn't want to call her back because I didn't want her to know that I had been drinking. *I have to get to her,* I told myself.

"Aye, bro, I gotta get to my girl. She's probably worried about me. She's been calling."

"A'ight, bro, thanks for coming out. You're not driving, are you?"

"Yea."

"Nah, homie, hold on. Let me get my keys."

"Nah, nigga, you just as drunk as me. I ain't fucking with you." I laughed.

"You right. I'm playing with you. I'll call you an uber."

"Nah, I'll be fine." I stumbled to my car.

~ ~ ~

I woke up the next day with my head pounding like crazy. I looked at the clock and saw it was almost eleven in the morning. I watched Keisha sleep. She was so beautiful. I hated the fact that we'd lost our baby. Dragging myself out of bed, I made her some breakfast, but she didn't eat much of anything.

~ ~ ~

Several days passed. Kiesha slept through most of them. I would make sure she was good and see if she wanted anything. Keisha didn't seem to appreciate my efforts but got mad at everything I did and said. I didn't know what to do. Two days ago, Keisha and I had our first argument.

She and I had never argued about anything before, I expressed how I felt about the miscarriage, and she seemed to have understood. After that she and I were doing well. We even made love, and that's something we hadn't done in months. We were finally moving forward with our relationship and moving on to planning our wedding. I couldn't be happier than to spend my life with a woman like her. She made me smile every time she walked into the room.

Felipe told me about a restaurant that he'd taken one of his girlfriends to. I'd heard many great things about it. Since Keisha and I were doing so well, I decided to surprise her and take her there. The day before, I went out and bought her a dozen red roses. Of course she loved them. As we were on our way to the restaurant, I could tell she was excited, and it was good to see her smiling again. *I have my girl back,* I told myself.

When we walked into the restaurant, we were both amazed at how beautiful the place was. I looked at Keisha and her eyes lit up with excitement. When our waitress came to the table, Keisha's smile disappeared. I'm pretty sure it was because the waitress was pregnant. Keisha went on to have a conversation with her, so I assumed everything was all good. But then she went to the restroom, and twenty minutes later she still hadn't come back. I asked Jessie if she could check on her for me, and I'm glad I did. Keisha had had a breakdown. I'd never seen her like that before and I was honestly scared.

The next morning, I woke up to make my beautiful future wife breakfast, but that didn't go so well. We had a huge argument that led to a breakup. When I walked out the door, I just wanted to turn back around and take her in my arms and never let her go, but something in me just couldn't do it. I was tired of being disrespected. It had crushed my heart when she took off the engagement ring. I was broken inside.

~ ~ ~

I stayed at my mom's house and lay in bed for a week straight. I called off sick from work, couldn't eat, couldn't sleep, and all I thought about was Keisha. I felt I was going half crazy. I wanted to call her so badly, but I didn't know what I could say to her. When my phone would ring, I'd hope it was her, but it never was. After two weeks of feeling sorry for myself, my mama came into my room to talk to me. I would always tell her I didn't want to talk, but this time she didn't care. She came in anyway.

"I can't believe that li'l bitch broke up with you and threw the engagement ring at you," Mom said angrily.

"Mom, don't call her that! She's just hurting inside," I shouted at my mom.

"Yeah, I know, but now my baby is hurting, and it breaks my heart to see you like this." Tears formed in her eyes. "I loved Keisha like a daughter, and I would've never thought she'd do this."

"I know, Ma."

"She must be really depressed." My mom's voice softened.

"She is. If you would have seen her, you wouldn't have recognized her. She cried all the time, and then she's loving, but she'll flip out on me just like that. I don't know what to do. I love her so much. I just want her to be OK."

"I know you do, baby." My mom sat on the edge of the bed. "I know what she's feeling. I've been there," she said sadly.

"What do you mean?"

"Um . . ." My mom tried to tell her story in between her tears. "I never told you this, but I lost a baby also. Three years before you were born, I got pregnant. Your father and I were so excited at first, but we were also very scared. You see, my father didn't want me dating a black man. He didn't want me dating anyone who wasn't Puerto Rican, but I loved him, and he loved me. When my father found out I was pregnant, he was so upset that he"— Mom paused and covered her mouth for a second—"he pushed me down the stairs. I hated him for that! Well, after your father saved up enough money, we got a place together and I moved out of my father's house." My mom sat a little taller and spoke with strength. "And I never turned back."

"I'm sorry, Mom. I love you." I sat up in bed.

"It's OK, baby, I love you more! Just give Keisha some time. They say if you love something you have to let it go, and if it comes back it means so much more, but if it doesn't . . . it's something you have to go through to grow."

"You're right. Thanks, Mom."

"You're welcome, baby." She kissed my forehead and walked away. "Oh, and get yo' ass up and in the shower. You stank."

I laughed. "OK, I will."

After my shower, my mind was still focused on Keisha, so I decided to go against my better judgement and give her a call. I dialed Keisha's phone number, but her mom answered and told me she was in the hospital in the psych ward.

My mind reeled. *My baby in the psych ward? I need to go see her.*

"Keisha didn't want me to tell you." She paused. "But she's been in the hospital for three days so far."

I had to go see my baby. I missed her so much. When I arrived at the hospital, I got turned away because they said she wasn't allowed to have any visitors, so I went back home and lay down and thought about her.

Maybe I can admit myself in the psych ward. At least I'd be able to see her, I thought to myself. I missed her so much it made me sick. I knew what I had to do, so I did something that I'd never done without Keisha by my side. I got down on my knees and looked to the Lord.

Lord, it's me, Hector. I'm not really good at this because Keisha always did the praying, and I always just listened. Lord, I come asking you to please watch over her, comfort her, guard her mind and keep her. Please help her to get over the miscarriage, and please don't allow her to go on with her life and still be bitter about it. Help her to understand that some things just happen, and we can't control them. I ask that you not only keep her but keep my mind also. It feels as if I'm going crazy at times without her. Watch over my thoughts.

God, I'm just going to put Keisha in your hands. I love her so much that I'm going to let her go. Please help me with this and give me the strength I need to move on without her for now, and when and if you bring her back to me, I promise to be the best man that I can be to her. In Jesus' name. Amen.

Grief Counseling

Keisha

I sat with others in a circle, listening to each person as they told their story about how they ended up here at The Grief House. I'd been at The Grief House for a week now, and I'd already opened up a lot. The people were really helpful. No one judged anyone for their actions, and everyone supported each other. I spoke with many women that were also grieving about different things. I even spoke with some men that were grieving.

During my one-on-one sessions, we talked about the main cause that brought me here. At first, I didn't want to open up about my miscarriage, but being here I learned that I had to be honest with myself. And being honest with myself meant that I had to be truthful. My counselor brought up three things. One of them threw me for a loop. I had no idea that I was still dealing with it.

1.) Miscarriage

After the miscarriage, the first thing that I felt was sadness. I was an emotional wreck. Then I felt ashamed and blamed myself as if it was my fault the miscarriage happened. I felt like less of a woman, because I couldn't give my future husband the baby that he was so excited to have. I also blamed God. I blamed Him because He allowed me to go through such a rough time. I felt angry, guilty, depressed, rage—so many emotions were going on inside my head.

During my session with the counselor, I learned that having the miscarriage wasn't my fault. One in four women experienced at least one miscarriage in their lifetime. I learned that a woman that had a miscarriage goes through many different emotions, and that was normal. I learned that it was OK to be sad, and it was OK to cry at times, but after a while, I should try to focus my attention on something else.

2.) Big Daddy

Big Daddy was the best man that ever came into my life. He gave me the unconditional love and support that I needed. I learned that because he was the one who was there for me and with me most of the time, I took out all my emotions on him, the good ones as well as the bad ones. I learned that instead of lashing out at him, I should have reached out to him while he was trying to reach out to me. I became so torn up over the miscarriage that I never even took his feelings into consideration. I pushed my future husband away from me, and I felt like shit because of it. I also learned that when a person was filled with so much emotion and they weren't in their right state of mind, sometimes it was best to walk away from the people that you love. I learned that overcoming grief was something that a person had to do on their own. You have to want it for yourself.

3.) Andy

I didn't think I would be in sessions talking about Andy. I figured that part of my life was over, and I'd blocked him out of my mind. He was dead to me. But I learned that even though he came into my life for such a short period of time, it made a huge impact. I learned that maybe I pushed Big Daddy away because deep down I wanted my father to treat me with the unconditional love and support that I never had from him. I did not want to talk about Andy at all. I felt more emotional talking about him than talking about the miscarriage. In my session, I broke down and told the truth about being a fatherless child.

Turns out, I was a daddy's girl all along. Even though he wasn't in my life, that's all I'd ever wanted to be. I learned that studies show that five times more fatherless girls become promiscuous and have a baby at a young age than girls that have a father in the home or in their life. I learned that my past behavior was a way of acting out and wanting my father in my life. I also learned that I had to accept things that had happened and things that were to come.

I had to accept the fact that I'd had a miscarriage. I had to accept the fact that Big Daddy and I were no longer together. And I had to accept Andy for who he was and who he had become. I learned that just because I accepted something didn't mean that I was over it. I was just learning how to live with it and learn to heal from it. During the session, the therapist suggested that I write a letter of forgiveness and also a letter apologizing to those that I'd hurt—which was Big Daddy and God. I had to forgive Andy for everything that had happened in the past, but mostly I had to forgive myself.

~ ~ ~

My time at The Grief House had me doing lots of soul searching. I'd never thought in a million years that I would turn away from God. I never thought that I wouldn't pray each day and thank Him for all that He had done for me. I felt ashamed, and I was embarrassed. I was certain that this was how Adam and Eve felt when they ate the forbidden fruit. I got down on my knees and cried out to the Lord.

Dear Lord, I come to you as humble as I know how. Lord, I ask that you forgive me for my sins, forgive me for turning my back on you. Lord, I'm sorry for not trusting in you. Please forgive me.

I clasped my hands together and spoke my prayer aloud. *Lord, I ask that you restore my faith. Help me to get my mind right. Lord, I ask that you create in me a clean heart, and renew a right spirit within me, within my mind, within my heart, and within my soul. Lord, I need your help. Help me to be a better mother, help me to become a better daughter, better sister, better friend. Help me to shine Your light everywhere I go. Lord, I ask that you watch over Big Daddy wherever he may be and whatever he may be doing. Lord, I'm sorry for the way I treated him. Please help me get better. I thank you in advance in Jesus' name. Amen,* I prayed.

After a month at The Grief House, I was now able to go home. I felt so much better. I felt normal again. I took the therapist's advice and decided to forgive myself as well as Andy. I might never see him again, but I now forgave him for everything he had put me through. I forgave myself and I promised myself that I would never go back to that state of mind again.

~ ~ ~

It had been six months since I left The Grief House. The first couple days were a bit tough because some nights I'd dream about being pregnant, and I'd wake up in a puddle of blood next to my dead baby. My mind played tricks on me through my dreams, so I attended meetings daily. As weeks went on, it got easier, and I only attended meetings once a week. I eventually stopped going. I prayed and asked God to renew my mind, and that's just what He did. I started going back to church on a regular basis like I had before, and things were falling into place for me. Jenny gave me a raise at work, and life was good.

I tried calling Big Daddy last month to see how he was doing. I hadn't heard from him since I'd been better. I wanted to apologize for the way things ended, but his phone was disconnected or maybe he'd changed his number. Either way, I couldn't worry about him. I had to move on with my life and focus on Li'l T and myself.

I hadn't been to a meeting in a couple of months, so my counselor called to check up on me and see how I was doing. She was glad to hear that I was on the right track, and she suggested that I volunteer to speak so that people could hear my story and learn how I was able to get my head together. I agreed.

~ ~ ~

I'd been volunteering at The Grief House for a month now and I loved it. The people there were like family. One particular woman, Shana, really stood out to me because she always asked me questions and told me how strong I was at such a young age. Shana was pretty, with pecan-brown skin, glamorous brown eyes, and high cheek bones. She was thick like Queen Latifah, but her perfect lips reminded me of Angelina Jolie's. I didn't know what she wore outside of The Grief House, but here she dressed like a bum and she never combed her hair. I knew how it was to feel down and out. Sometimes it took so much out of a person just to get out of bed and nobody understood.

"Hey, Keisha." Shana walked up behind me.

"Hey, Shana. How are you doing today?" I asked.

"I'm making it. I wish I was more like you, Keisha. You are so beautiful, and it's like you never let anything bother you." Shana looked sad.

"I'm glad I don't look like what I've been through. But have you been listening to anything I've been saying this last month? I was messed up, bad. I lost my mind, I lost my fiancé, I was in a place in my life where I didn't want to live anymore, and I felt like there was no point in going on. But thank God for Jesus. He restored my mind and I know it was nobody but Him that kept me. He placed me here with some amazing counselors that talked to me and allowed me to dig deep within myself. I'm happy I decided to take that step and come here, because if I didn't, I'd probably still be lost."

"I love it when you come here. You always make me feel so much better," Shana replied with a smile.

"I'm glad I can help." I smiled back.

"There's something I've been meaning to ask you."

"What's up, beautiful?" I asked.

"Do you really think I'm beautiful?" she asked with tears forming in her eyes.

"Of course! You are! You were made in His image and His likeness, and God creates nothing but the best." I wiped the tears from her cheeks.

"Can you be my sponsor?" Shana blurted out.

"Ahhhh." I was at a loss for words. I didn't know exactly what the roll of a sponsor entailed, but I didn't want to let her down. "Sure."

"Thank you, thank you!" She hugged me tightly.

Memories

I sat outside on the porch on the nice sunny day, enjoying the summer weather. Li'l T played outside with his toys. He played so well by himself. I'd been sponsoring Shana for the past four months, and it was actually going pretty well. She had her own place now, and I saw a positive change in her from the way she acted in the beginning to the way she acted now. She was a very beautiful woman. She did her make up every day and her hair was always styled. Shana had come to church with me a few times. She told me that she'd been dating a guy that used to live in her building, so I didn't hear from her as much as I used to, but I still called and checked up on her every few days.

~ ~ ~

Li'l T and I were out grocery shopping for the week when I heard someone yelling my name. When I looked back and saw who had called out my name, I was speechless, and my heart began to beat faster and faster. Li'l T took off running into his arms, and they hugged each other for an entire minute before they let go.

"Hey, Keisha, how are you doing?" Big Daddy said, leaning in for a hug.

"I'm fine and you?" I replied as I inhaled his fresh scent.

"I'm good. I just bought a new house."

"Wow! That's amazing. I'm happy for you. Congratulations." I smiled.

"Thank you, thank you, I appreciate it." He smiled back.

"I tried calling you, but I guess your phone was disconnected."

"I got a new number."

"Oh." I was a bit dispirited.

"So how is your mom doing?" he asked.

"She's good. How about your mom?"

"She good. So, tell me, how are you really doing, Keisha?" he gazed into my eyes the way he did when we were together.

"I'm good, really. I'm better. I'm back into church and my mind isn't in that dark place it was before." I smiled.

"That's what's up. I was praying for you," Big Daddy said.

"I appreciate that. You know when I called you, I was calling to apologize for how things went down. I never meant for them to be that way."

"It's coo' girl. I'm just glad you're better." He hugged me again.

"Can you take me to get ice cream?" Li'l T asked, tapping Big Daddy's leg.

"Do you still have the same number?" Big Daddy asked me.

"Yes, I do." I nodded my head.

"There you are. I've been looking all over for you." Up walked a gorgeous Latina woman with long black curly hair and glowing skin. Her red lipstick brought out the fullness of her lips, and her makeup was on point, almost better than Shana's. She looked to have been at least six months pregnant.

"You know I wasn't far," Big Daddy replied to her and then they kissed on the lips. "This is Keisha. Keisha, this is Sophie." Big Daddy introduced us.

"Nice to meet you," I said, but then I grabbed Li'l T's hand and turned to go. "Li'l T, come on, let's go."

"It was nice seeing you, Keisha. I'll hit you up." Big Daddy called out.

"OK." I walked away with mixed emotions. I was happy to see Big Daddy, but I didn't know he'd moved on. A part of me thought how that was supposed to be my baby and how Big Daddy was supposed to be my man. But I said my peace to him, and now I had to go on with my life. *But did he just really introduce me to his pregnant girlfriend?* I asked myself, happy to be moving on with my life now.

"Mommy, can we get some ice cream?" Li'l T asked.

"Yes, baby, but first we have to go home so we can put the groceries up."

~ ~ ~

Later that night, as I sat relaxing and flipping through channels on the TV, I got a call from an unknown phone number.

"Hello?" I answered.

"What's up, Keisha."

I recognized the voice. "I just tucked Li'l T into bed. I didn't expect to hear from you so soon."

"Yeah, I know it was a bit awkward earlier, and I wanted to apologize for that," Big Daddy said.

"There's no need to apologize. You moved on. And that's to be expected." There was silence on the phone. "Well, congratulations on the baby, and I'd appreciated it if you didn't call me anymore. Have a nice life." I slammed the phone down. I understood why he'd moved on, but he didn't have to call me. I got ready for bed as I listened to "Dissed Him" by En Vogue.

The next morning, I woke up to someone banging on my door.

"Who is it?" I yelled as I made my way to the front door.

"It's me, girl, open the door."

I recognized Shana's voice, so I opened the door. As soon as I opened it, she pushed past me as if I wasn't even standing there and made her way into my house.

"Get dressed, girl. Let's go to breakfast."

"It's Saturday. I just wanna sleep in for once."

"Girl, you can sleep when your dead. Now get dressed. My man gave me some money and I wanna take you out to say thank you because you've done so much for me, and you helped me get on the right track."

"Well, since your man is paying for it, I guess. Oh, and just to let you know, I will be ordering a big man's meal." I laughed.

Shana laughed. "Do you want me to get Li'l T dressed and ready?"

"Yes, that'll be great if you can."

~ ~ ~

Shana and I spent the entire day together. After breakfast we went to the nail shop and got manicures and pedicures, then we went shopping, and afterwards to dinner. We had a great time. I not only became Shana's sponsor, but I became her friend too. She was a joy to be around and she was super funny.

"I had fun today." Shana took her eyes off the road and glanced at me.

"Yeah, me too," I smiled, looking back at her. "Are you coming to church tomorrow?"

"Yes, I'll be there. I've been trying to get my man to come, but we'll see if he does." She pulled into my driveway and shifted into park.

"Alright, girl, I'll see you tomorrow." I got out of Shana's car.

"Alright, girl."

Li'l T and I walked into the house. He went straight for the TV, and I began to settle in when there was a knock at my door. I figured it was Shana again.

What does she want now? I asked myself.

"Open the door for Shana, Li'l T," I yelled.

"Yes, ma'am," Li'l T replied.

I continued to put my clothes away when I heard a man's voice. I ran to the living room to see who was in my house and when I got there, I was shocked.

"Mommy, Big Daddy came to take me for ice cream."

"Oh, he did?" I gave Big Daddy a mean mug.

"I said if it was OK with your mom we could go." Big Daddy looked at me and smiled. He looked so sexy. He had a fresh haircut and his lineup was on point. Seeing him smile at me like that brought me back to when we were together. He used to stare at me, and when I'd catch him staring, he'd smile and tell me how beautiful I was. I wanted to hug and kiss him and let him know just how much I've missed him.

"Shouldn't you be with your baby mama?" I asked.

"I don't have a baby mama."

"You don't have to play games with me, Hector."

"I'm not playing games with you, girl. Look, let's take Li'l T to get some ice cream and I'll explain everything."

"OK."

We went to get ice cream and sat at the park so that Li'l T could play while Big Daddy and I talked. Li'l T had Big Daddy pushing him on the swing most of the time, so we didn't do much talking. It was beginning to get dark outside, so we headed back to my house. We had a long day and Li'l T hadn't had a nap, so I was sure he was tired. I gave him a bath and tucked him in for the night.

"Li'l T must've been tired; he went to sleep before we got him in bed good," Big Daddy said.

"Yeah, we were out most of the day before you showed up." I walked into the living room.

"So, can we talk now?" he followed me.

"Talk." I folded my arms.

"Look, Keisha, it's been almost a year and I've thought about you each and every day. You hurt me bad. You were supposed to be my wife, and when you took off the engagement ring and tripped out on me, it really fucked me up. You was my first girlfriend, and I wanted you to be my last. I tried to be there for you the best way that I could, and you continued to push me back each time. I get it that you were hurt, well I was too, but we should've supported each other."

"You're right. I'm sorry, Big Daddy." I unfolded my arms and took his hands. "I was in a real messed up state of mind, and I want to apologize for hurting you the way I did. You didn't deserve it. I hope you can find it in your heart to forgive me," I sincerely said.

"I wouldn't be here if I didn't." He smiled.

"Don't be smiling at me like that. Shouldn't you be with your girlfriend anyway?" I asked.

"I don't have a girlfriend. Sophie is Felipe's cousin. Last month she seen me over his house. We were all drinking—well, not her—but I remember that I was only talking about how I missed you. Sophie listened to me talk about you for hours until she thought she'd get my mind off you. Well, one thing led to another and we went all the way."

I made a face, a bit shocked and disappointed.

"The baby isn't mine. She was already pregnant. Her dude went to prison, and she and I been hanging out here and there. The day we saw you at the store, she knew who you were from pictures that I had shown her. I didn't think she'd be petty and kiss me, but she did. You know I don't do any drama, but when we got into the car, I told her she was out of line doing that. After she cussed me out, I dropped her off at her house and that was that. I hadn't spoken to her since, and I only thought about you since then."

"Oh, wow. So, you had sex with a pregnant chick. Did y'all use protection?" I asked, concerned.

"Come on now, Keisha, you know me better than that."

"Did you?" I asked again.

"Of course, we did. I wouldn't have hit it if I didn't have protection," Big Daddy said seriously. "Enough about her. Look, I don't know what the future has in store for us, but I let you get away once, and I'm not gonna do it again."

"And how do you know that I don't have a man?" I rolled my neck.

"Come on now, Keisha, if you had a man, I wouldn't be here right now. You're a good woman. You're not like that." He smiled at me again, only this time he licked his bottom lip.

I wasn't sure if he knew how much he was turning me on right now.

"You don't know what I'm like anymore." I rolled my eyes.

"You're right, I don't. But you can tell me." Big Daddy moved even closer to me.

My heart was racing. I hadn't been with anyone since I'd last been with him. Before I knew it, Big Daddy's lips were on mine and our tongues danced with each other for at least five minutes without taking a break. His hands roamed my body until I pushed him back.

"I'm sorry, Keisha." Big Daddy stepped back and lifted his hands.

"Don't apologize, Big Daddy. We both were into it. Honestly, I missed you so much too. When I got better and tried to call you, I was heartbroken that your number was disconnected. I wanted to stop at your mom's house many times, but I just couldn't bring myself to do it. I still love you and I hate the way I treated you."

"It's cool, girl. I got you." He hugged me tight.

Big Daddy and I sat on my bed and talked about what life was like without each other for the past several months. I told him about my stay at The Grief House and the things that I'd learned from my counselors. I told him how I was sponsoring Shana and how I'd had no idea what I was doing at first. He told me how he'd missed me and wanted to call me several times but didn't because he thought I'd flip out in him. Big Daddy told me how he never stopped praying for me.

We also talked about how he wanted to go to church, but he didn't know how that would look since he and I weren't together anymore. I told him that he should never be afraid to go into the Lord's house because we are all welcome.

"It's almost four in the morning." I glanced at the cable box.

"Damn, I hadn't noticed. I could talk to you all night, girl."

"I could too, but I have to be at Sunday School at eight in the morning."

"Do you mind if I come to church with you?" Big Daddy asked.

"Of course not. But maybe you should take your car. I don't want anyone getting the wrong idea."

"I feel you. Look, Keisha, I meant what I said. I'm not letting you get away this time without fighting for you. I didn't fight hard enough for you the last time, but this time I have my game face on. I am willing to do whatever it takes for you and me to make this work. I love you, girl."

I smiled, thinking over what he said. "Well, maybe we can take it slow, without rushing into anything. We've spent months apart and I'm sure we've changed in some areas. I'm not saying that I'm your girlfriend as of yet, but I am open to it if you are."

"Say no more, girl. I'll do whatever you want me to do."

"Whatever I want you to do?" I asked.

"Whatever you want me to do." He repeated.

"Well, right now I want you to make like a banana and split so I can get some sleep for a couple hours." I laughed.

He laughed too. "You are so corny, but a'ight, girl. I'll see you in the morning." Big Daddy hugged me and kissed my cheek.

Together Again

I sat on the couch as Li'l T and Big Daddy play-wrestled each other. It had been a month since Big Daddy and I decided that we would take things slow. Since then, we'd been spending every day together. We rode to church together instead of separately. I felt like things had returned to how they used to be between us. He made me fall more in love with him each day, even by him doing the smallest things. He would randomly buy flowers for me, or when I would start cooking, he would finish and tell me to sit down.

Big Daddy, Li'l T, and I were baking cookies when I received a call from Shana.

"Well-well-well, I haven't heard from you in a while. What's up, girl?" I said.

"Keisha." Shana said my name as if she'd been crying.

"What's wrong? Are you OK?" I walked out of the kitchen so that I could hear Shana better.

"It's my boyfriend. We got into an argument, and he slapped me. I told him to leave, but he won't. I don't wanna call the police on him because I don't want him to go to jail."

"I'm on my way!" I ended the call and grabbed my keys.

"Hey, Big Daddy, that was Shana. She needs me right now. Can you keep an eye on Li'l T?"

"Yeah, of course, girl."

"Thank you." I kissed both him and Li'l T on the cheek before heading for the door.

When I arrived at Shana's apartment, I saw two cop cars parked outside. *I hope she's OK,* I said to myself as I rushed to her door. Before I had a chance to knock, she opened the door.

"Are you OK? I saw the police cars," I asked as I walked right past her and into her house.

"I'm fine. The police are at the apartment across the hall. I was watching through the peep hole," Shana replied with her head held down.

I grabbed her chin and lifted her face.

"Oh my God, did he do this to you?" I barely recognized my beautiful friend. She looked like Angela Bassett playing Tina Turner after Ike beat her in the 1993 film *What's Love Got to Do with It?*

"Yes." Shana broke down crying.

I held onto her and cried with her. It was tough seeing a friend in this situation.

"Where is that bastard?" I asked, feeling enraged.

"He left when he seen the police outside. He thought I called them on him."

"Shana, I know you don't want to hear this, but he needs to be in jail!" I spoke, reassuring her. "No man should EVER put their hands on a woman! Have you seen your face?"

"No, I haven't." She silently cried.

I stood her up and walked her over to the mirror hanging on the living room wall. "Look!" I lifted her head and she stared back at herself. "Now, do you think that nigga deserves to be free, out living his best life while you're all fucked up? You're a beautiful woman, and you don't deserve any of this. I'm mad as hell that this happened to you," I spat furiously.

"What should I do?" Shana asked.

"Call the police!" I looked out the window to see if the police cars were still outside, but they were gone. I pulled out my cell phone and held it out for Shana.

She hesitantly grabbed it from my hand, but she dialed 9-1-1. "They're sending someone," Shana said as she gave me my cell phone back.

"OK, good. Now go and pack a bag, because you're staying at my house for a couple days. I don't want that bastard trying to come back here, in case the police don't catch him right away."

"OK." Just as she headed to her room, someone knocked at the door.

We both walked towards the door, without asking who it was or looking through the peep hole because we knew the police were on the way. I opened the door, and when I saw Andy standing on the other side, I froze up and my heart began to beat faster and faster. The three of us stood there for a minute straight without saying anything to each other: me, Shana, and my dad.

"What are you doing here?" I broke the silence.

"I came to speak with my woman!" he said rudely. "What are you doing here?"

"This is the man that did this to you?" I asked Shana. She hesitantly shook her head yes, and I became furious all over again. "You're a monster! What kinda 'man' would do this to a woman?" I asked in rage.

Instead of replying to me, he turned his attention to Shana.

"Shana, baby, I'm sorry." He spoke sympathetically. "Can I come in so we can talk about this?"

"No!" I answered for her.

"This has nothing to do with you. Why don't you stay in a child's place?" He pointed his finger in my direction.

"This has EVERYTHING to do with me because I'm her friend, and just to let you know I called the police and they're on the way!" I folded my arms. "I hope yo' ass rot in jail, you bastard!"

"Fuck you, bitch."

I couldn't reply. Deep down I wanted to bash his head into the wall until he could no longer breathe. But the God in me didn't allow that to happen, so I let the tears fall instead.

"Hi, folks, we received a call of an assault," one of two policemen said. He strode down the hallway of Shana's apartment as we stood inside the doorway.

"No, it was all just a misunderstanding, but we're good now." Andy said before either Shana or I had a chance to speak.

"Is this true, miss?" asked the officer.

"How about you see for yourself?" I moved Shana up closer so the officers could see her face.

"Officer, this is my girlfriend. My daughter called me and told me that someone had jumped on my girlfriend, and I was coming over to see what was going on. Right, Keisha?" Andy asked.

I looked at Shana, and she looked at me. I could tell that she didn't want him to go to jail.

"Yeah, that's true officer," I lied. Andy was my dad and I didn't want anything bad happening to him, even if he disrespected me and Shana.

"Do you know who did this to you, ma'am?" the same officer asked Shana.

She didn't reply, she just shook her head "no" with shame.

Shana was a very attractive woman, but right now she wasn't, and this was all my father's doing. I looked at her black eye, her busted lip, and blue and purple cheeks. I couldn't let this man get away with it, even if he was my father.

"Officer," I spoke up. "Yes, this is my father, and yes this is his girlfriend, but he's the one that did this to her." Tears ran down my face. I loved Shana as if she were a sister to me, and I wasn't gonna allow a man to do this to her and get away with it, no matter who he was.

"Really, Keisha? I'm your father, and you snitched on me?" Andy yelled as the police arrested him.

"Actually, a father is someone that takes care of his child. When have you ever taken care of me? You came into my life and ruined it! I hate you!" I cried out as he got arrested.

As Shana and I packed her bag to stay at my house, she kept apologizing because she'd had no idea that Andy was my father. I never mentioned his name to her, and she always referred to him as her man, so neither of us had a clue they were the same man. We both agreed that he needed to pay for what he had done to her. Maybe sitting in jail would teach him to think twice before he put his hands on another woman. Before we went to my house, we stopped at the police station to fill out all the necessary paperwork.

Lord, forgive me! I know I told Andy that I hate him, but I was really upset, and I didn't mean it. Help me to forgive him and move on with my life. Lord, help me to not hold onto the past but help me move on towards the future and not look back anymore. Lord, I thank you once again, in Jesus' name, Amen.

Moving Forward

I was home making dinner for my men. Big Daddy would soon come home from work, so I wanted to have it ready for him. A week had gone by since Andy's arrest. Shana decided not to press charges, so he was released from jail. Since he'd been out, he'd been calling both Shana and me like crazy. Shana decided that it would be best if she moved in with a relative, because she was afraid Andy would come back to the house. I agreed with her.

As I was finishing up dinner, Andy's number popped up on my screen. *Lord, help me to say the right things, without being angry. Lord, help him to talk to me with respect.*

"Hello," I answered after I took a deep breath.

"Hi, young lady, it's me, your dad."

"My dad?" I questioned. "You mean Andy. Yeah, what's up?"

"I just wanted to apologize for the way I treated you and for calling you out of your name. That was uncalled for. I understand why you did what you did. Honestly, I would have done it too. I wanted to ask if it would be OK if I came over or if we could go somewhere fun, you know, like old times."

The little girl inside of me jumped up and down for joy. That little girl was super excited to hear her father say those words. But the woman in me knew he was full of it, and I couldn't allow myself to get hurt by him anymore. But instead of turning down his proposal, I had other plans in mind.

"Sure. Meet me tomorrow at 1234 West Street at three in the afternoon. I'll be in Suite 33. Don't be late." I gave him the address of my counselor's office, the one that I'd met at The Grief House.

"OK, I'll be there. I promise."

"Honestly, I don't go by what a person says but by what a person does," I said nonchalantly.

"I understand. Well, I will see you at three tomorrow."

"OK."

~ ~ ~

I arrived at my counselors' office at 2:00 p.m. so that I could talk to her before Andy showed up. She told me to just be myself, let out everything that I needed to let out, and ask questions, even the hard one's that I was afraid to ask. She assured me that everything was going to be OK and that this might be just the breakthrough that I needed to move on with my life.

"Mrs. Jones, I have your three o'clock here to see you," said my counselor's assistant as she paged into the room.

"OK, send him in." Mrs. Jones looked at me, seeing my reaction.

"Hi, Mr. Moore. Come in and have a seat. My name is Mrs. Jones, and I've been counseling Ra'Keisha for some time now. Ra' Keisha thought it'd be a good idea for you all to sit down and talk about some things. Are you OK with that?" Mrs. Jones asked Andy.

"Um, I don't know. Do you want me to stay, young lady?" Andy looked at me.

"I don't want you to do anything you don't want to do. You called me, wanting to meet," I said with my head up.

"You're right. I'll stay, and we can discuss anything you want." Andy sat down and made himself comfortable on the love seat.

"Ra' Keisha, let's start with you. Why don't you tell Andy how you feel?" Mrs. Jones said.

I had so much that I wanted to say, and I had so many unanswered questions, but in that moment, I became a mute.

"Ra' Keisha." Mrs. Jones spoke. "How did it feel when you first met Andy?"

"When I first met Andy, honestly, I was in shock and didn't know how to even feel. But after the first time we hung out, I was ecstatic! We did so many fun things together and we had a great time. It was everything I'd ever wanted and more. I felt like I was a kid and Andy was just being that great father that he always had been. But suddenly it all had changed, and I no longer heard from Andy. He started ignoring my calls as well as my texts."

"I wasn't sure if I had done something wrong, but I blamed myself." I started to get teary eyed. "My mom has been there for me through EVERYTHING, and when she called to hang out with me and Li'l T, I turned her away because I was with you, Andy." I sobbed because of the way I'd treated my mother.

"Andy, do you have anything that you want to say?" asked Mrs. Jones.

Andy took a deep breath before speaking.

"I didn't know you felt that way, young lady. I know I started to become distant from you, but that was because, like you said, you had your mom. She's been there for you all of your life, so I felt like I couldn't just come in and take you away from her."

"You weren't taking me away from her," I replied, wondering if he was telling the truth or just saying that because I mentioned my mother.

"But I was. I can tell how close you and your mom are, and I know she was upset when you chose to hang out with me instead of her. But honestly that day when you chose your mom over me, that hurt me deeply and I felt like I could never compete with that because you're always gonna choose her over me," Andy stated. "I'm the type of person that don't come in second to no one," he said in a cocky way.

I didn't understand his explanation and hurt. How dare he say he was hurt, when he's hurt me since he came into my life and gave me false hope. Hearing him say that, I realized that I had to do something for me to move on with my life and heal from this situation. During the session, we also talked about his childhood and how his father had walked out of his life, but he'd had an amazing stepfather, who died and again left him. He shed a few tears as he talked about his father, and I saw that he really cared. It made me wonder how he could do the same thing to me if he knew the pain it caused.

"Well, we've come to the end of our session. Do either of you have anything else that you would like to say?" asked Mrs. Jones.

"Young lady"—Andy leaned forward in the seat—"I'm glad that you allowed me to come here with you today, and I hope we can move on from everything that happened in the past and move towards the future. I'll be a better father to you and a better grandfather to li'l man."

"Li'l man, huh? Do you even know my son's name?" Tears rolled down my face. "Honestly, since you came into my life, I haven't been the same. Do you remember Thanksgiving Day?"

"Look, I'm sorry about that. I know I said some things that I shouldn't have said."

"I remember that day like it was yesterday. You told me that you didn't have time for me, and to stop calling you, and to stay out of your life, but you wanna know the most hurtful thing that you said to me? You told me that I wasn't your daughter!" I sobbed. "Do you know that I had a breakdown because of that?"

"I'm sorry," he said.

"But you know what? I think you're right about something, we should definitely put the past behind us."

"Thank you, young lady." Andy smiled.

"I took you into my home and cared for you, and you hurt me again." I huffed. "But I think we should move on with our lives and forget about each other. I'm happy with my life now and you're not in it. I wish you well, and may God bless you." I stood up and walked out.

The drive home felt good. I finally got the closure that I needed in order to move past all the hurt that I had endured from Andy.

The Mrs.

I was lying in Big Daddy's arms as we watched the TV show *Power* starring Omari Hardwick. His best friend Tommy, played by Joseph Sikora, had just found out who his real father was. During each episode, he and his father became close and did things together for fun. My mind turned to Andy. Two months had gone by since the session with Mrs. Jones and Andy. I hadn't heard from him since, but my life was going good without him. Big Daddy and I were doing great, our relationship better than ever.

~ ~ ~

I was in the living room, folding clothes when Big Daddy walked in.

"I got you this dress to wear to church on Sunday. Do you like it?" Big Daddy came into the room and held up a beautiful white and gold lace gown.

"Yeah, it's very nice and elegant. Thank you, babe, but you didn't have to buy me anything. I could have worn something from my closet."

"I know I didn't have to, girl, but I wanted to. Oh, and I made you an appointment to get your hair done tomorrow at five o'clock."

"OK," I said with a confused look on my face. "But why, what's wrong with my hair?"

"I'm taking you to this one spot afterwards, and we gotta dress up," Big Daddy replied.

"OK, babe." I threw my hand up at him. "Where are we going that we have to dress up?"

"Don't worry about it. Do you trust me?" He gazed into my eyes.

"Yes." I smiled, remembering the last time he asked me that.

"Do you love me?" he asked

"Yes."

"A'ight then, that's all I want you to do, girl."

"Whatever you say."

"Whatever I say, huh? Well, I say bring them lips here, girl."

Without replying, I did what I was told and kissed Big Daddy on the lips.

~ ~ ~

Two minutes went by, and I was still looking at myself in the mirror, admiring the gown that Big Daddy had gotten for me to wear to church today. It looked great on me and it was the perfect fit. My hair was silk pressed and fixed up into a perfect bun. I was stunning! I looked over-dressed for a Sunday morning church service, but Big Daddy insisted I wear it.

Big Daddy and Li'l T stepped out of the other room, and they looked amazing. They wore matching white suits, each with a gold vest underneath. They were sharp.

"Damn, girl! You fine as hell!" Big Daddy said, walking over to me.

"Me? Look at you. If I wasn't going to church, I'd be ready to do something else to you instead." I winked at him.

"Is that right?"

"Yeah, that's right, Big Daddy." I kissed him on the lips.

"Mommy, look at me." Li'l T opened his jacket up.

"You look so handsome, baby. Let me get my camera so that I can take a picture of my men."

"My mom is coming to church with us. I'll pick her up on the way there," Big Daddy said.

"Wow! She coming too?" I was shocked because Ms. Marrero had never come to church with us before.

"Yeah, she wanted to come," Big Daddy replied.

"Cool."

We walked into the church. It was nicely decorated with flowers and bows on the pews. I wondered what was going on because I'd never seen the church look this good before. I noticed that mostly everyone in church was over dressed, even people that hardly ever dressed up.

We took our usual seats. It seemed like church service moved rather quickly today because Bishop Bernard was already preaching, and it was only eleven thirty. Just before Bishop Bernard was about to give the benediction to dismiss the church, he called Big Daddy up to the altar.

What's going on here? I asked myself. I glanced over at my mom, and she had the biggest smile on her face. I looked at Big Daddy's mom and she was crying.

"Ra' Keisha, can you come up here with me?" Big Daddy said into the microphone.

I looked around, confused as could be, but I stood up and made my way to the altar with Big Daddy. *What is going on? Why did Bishop give him the microphone and call him up there? He's not a preacher,* I said to myself.

"Ra' Keisha." Big Daddy took my hand. "I was a fool when I let you get away from me before. I should've fought for you harder, but I'm not gonna dwell on that. I wanna focus on our now and focus on our future, our future together! Keisha, I can't picture my life without you. When we were apart, all I wanted was to be with you." Big Daddy dropped down on one knee. "I wanna build a family with you. You are all I want, and you are all I need. I love you, girl. I guess what I'm tryna say is, will you marry me?"

My eyes watered and my heart began to speed up. I loved this man with all my heart. He's all that I thought of and all that I dreamed of. There was only one thing for me to say.

"Yes! Yes, I will marry you," I replied as tears streamed down my face.

Big Daddy stood up and kissed my lips.

"Will you marry me now?" Big Daddy asked into the microphone.

"Now?" I asked confused. "What do you mean, now?"

"Keisha, I don't wanna go another day without you being my wife. I can't wait any longer. So what do you say?" Big Daddy asked.

"Yes." I nodded, crying hysterically. I couldn't believe he had done all of this. He was definitely the man that I wanted to spend the rest of my life with. *Thank you, God, for sending him my way.*

We had twenty minutes to get things ready. Big Daddy hired someone to do my make-up. He'd hired a photographer. His little cousin was the flower girl, and Li'l T the ring bearer. Shana, Quesha, and my sister were the bridesmaids. My brother, Felipe, and another one of Big Daddy's friends were the groomsmen. Bishop Bernard officiated the wedding.

Big Daddy had thought of everything and all I had to do was show up, and of course say yes!

~ ~ ~

After our wedding, Big Daddy and I had our pictures taken at the lake under the gazebo. Afterwards, we headed to a hall that he'd rented, where the rest of our family set things up for the reception. At the reception, we ate some wonderful food, from Spanish food to soul food. We danced and had a great time the entire night.

"Are you enjoying yourself?" Big Daddy asked as we slow danced to "Spend My Life with You" by Eric Benet, featuring Tamia.

"Of course, I am, baby. I can't believe you did all this! You are such an incredible man; I love you so much! I will never forget this day. You've made all my dreams come true, and you're everything and more that I prayed for in a man. I truly appreciate you, Big Daddy." A tear fell from my eye.

"I love you more, girl, and you already know that I appreciate you, but there's something that I have to tell you."

"What's up?" I asked my husband.

"We have to get going because we have to catch a flight."

"What do you mean?" I asked.

"We can't get married and not have a honeymoon. Our bags are already packed and in the car. All we have to do is get to the airport." Big Daddy grinned, looking pleased with all his surprises.

I stood there with my mouth open, trying to process the fact that Big Daddy had asked me to marry him, and thirty minutes later I was his wife, and now we're going on a honeymoon. This all happened within hours.

"How did you do all of this?" I asked in shock.

"We can talk about all that later. We should get going."

"What about Li'l T?" I asked.

"Do you trust me?" He gazed into my eyes.

"Of course I do, husband." It felt good saying the word husband.

"It's all taken care of, girl. Now let's thank everyone for coming so we can get outta here." Big Daddy kissed my lips.

Big Daddy was the man of my dreams. He was my soul mate, the man that had my heart, and now he was the man that I would spend the rest of my life with. I couldn't be happier.

Married Life

I was home folding laundry, thinking about how my life had changed over the course of a year. I loved being Mrs. Marrero, and my life had been nothing more than amazing since then. Li'l T and I moved out of my house and moved in with Big Daddy, but he only had a two-bedroom house, and eight months ago, I found out that I was pregnant. With the baby coming, we needed something larger, so we were saving up to purchase our first home together.

We found out that we were having a baby girl. Big Daddy was so excited to be having a baby that he'd helped create that he went out and bought a ton of baby clothes, bottles, diapers, and wipes. I was upset because we hadn't yet had the baby shower, and we didn't know what everyone was going to buy. We also still had the stuff that we got when he gave me the surprise party.

~ ~ ~

"Hey, babe, what's up?" I answered the phone on the third ring.

"What's up, girl? I'm on my way home, but I need you to get dressed because I am taking you and Li'l T out to eat," Big Daddy said into the phone.

"OK, I hope you aren't close by. You know I'm almost nine months pregnant and I don't move as fast as I used to."

"Just do what you can do, and when I get there, I'll help you."

"OK, babe, see you soon."

"A'ight, girl. I love you." Big Daddy said.

"I love you more." I hung up the phone and attempted to start getting dressed.

~ ~ ~

"Did y'all enjoy dinner?" asked Big Daddy as we walked out of the restaurant.

"Yes, I want more," Li'l T said from the back seat.

"You didn't even finish your plate, Li'l T," I said.

"Because I was full."

"So, now you're hungry again?" I asked Li'l T.

"Yes." He laughed.

I couldn't help but to laugh at him too. "Dinner was great, babe, thanks," I said to Big Daddy.

"Anything for my family." He lifted my hand that he was already holding and kissed the back of it as he drove. "Do you mind if I make a stop real quick?"

"Well, I hope there's a bathroom wherever it is because I have to use it."

"OK, we're almost there. You can choose which bathroom you like the most," he said with a smile.

"What do you mean?" I asked.

"You'll see." Big Daddy kissed the back of my hand once more.

We turned onto Venice Creek, a well-kept street with beautiful homes. We pulled into the driveway of a nice two-story colonial home with fancy columns on the porch.

"Who lives here?" I asked.

"Come on. Let's go look inside." Big Daddy came to my side of the car and opened the door for me.

"Who lives here, babe?" I asked again.

Big Daddy ignored me once again, pulled a key out of his pocket, and opened the front door.

"Big Daddy, who's house is this?" I asked, annoyed because he wasn't answering me.

"Well, first, go use the bathroom, then look around and tell me if you like it or not. If you do, then it's yours," Big Daddy stated nonchalantly.

"What do you mean, mine?" I asked as my eyes got wider.

"Just what I said, girl, if you like it, then it's yours."

Tears began to stream down my face. I was already emotional, and Big Daddy always seemed to amaze me. He always went above and beyond for me and Li'l T.

"What's wrong, girl, why are you crying?" he asked me.

"When did you have time to buy a house?" I sobbed. "I thought we were going to wait until after the baby was born?"

"I know, baby, but I didn't want you to worry about anything. I want our baby to come to our home when she leaves the hospital."

"You are so good to me."

"Nah, girl, we're good to each other. Now come on and let's check out the place." Big Daddy grabbed my hand and led the way.

The house was everything that I had wanted. Big Daddy and I often had talks about what we wanted our home to be like. I was most amazed at the bathroom. I always told him that I wanted my own bathroom, and he gave me just that. Our master bedroom was everything. It had a walk-in closet, and inside the closet was the master bathroom with a jacuzzi tub, marble head shower, a double sink, and a vanity set connected.

"Oh my God, babe, I can't believe you did this!" I hugged Big Daddy.

"Well, believe it, girl."

"Why do we need five bedrooms though?"

"Well, me and you, Li'l T, baby Marrero, and a guest bedroom."

"That's only four. We have another entire bedroom."

"Honestly, girl, I was thinking that maybe after we have this baby, you'd wanna have another one." He kissed my forehead.

"You're being serious, aren't you?" I asked.

"Dead ass."

"Big Daddy, I haven't even had this baby yet, and you're already talking about having another one. I have to think about that, babe. I'm not sure if that's something I just wanna jump right into. We still have to find a babysitter and stuff for this baby when I go back to work."

"Who says you have to work?" Big Daddy blurted out. "I make enough money now so that you don't have to work. You're only working three days a week anyway, Kiesha."

I propped my hands on my hips and stood staring at him. "Well, it looks like you have my life all planned out, huh?"

"That's not what I meant, girl, and you know it."

"Whatever." I flung my hand up and turned away. "I'll be in the car." I walked away from him.

No one spoke on the drive home. I was upset because he wanted me to be a stay-at-home mom. It had worked out fine back when we were younger, but now that I was older and I made my own money, I didn't want to just sit at home and have kids. In Big Daddy's family, the women stayed home and raised the kids while their husbands worked. I knew we had some cultural differences, but he married a black woman, and we need to discuss these things before just assuming it would be OK.

When we got home, I gave Li'l T a bath and tucked him into bed because he had to go to school in the morning. I went to our room and lay down. A few minutes later, Big Daddy walked in. He didn't say a word. Instead, he crawled into bed next to me and made me forget the reason that I was even mad at him.

"Keisha," Big Daddy said as I lay on his chest, "I'm sorry about earlier. I wasn't trying to upset you or anything. I just thought that since we were married now, you'd want to have more kids, and instead of paying a babysitter, you could stay home and raise the kids while I work. All of my aunts are stay-at-home moms, and so are my cousins."

"It's OK, baby. But I think that's something that we should have discussed first before you assumed that. Just because some of the members of your family are stay-at-home moms, doesn't mean that I want to be one."

"OK, I will support whatever you wanna do girl because I love you."

"I love you too, Big Daddy."

~ ~ ~

Two weeks later, we were all settled into our new home. I loved everything about it! The neighborhood was nice and quiet, and our neighbors were friendly. At first, I didn't know how the neighbors would react to a black family living on their street, because I'd only seen Caucasians around, but they were really friendly and welcoming. The family next door even told us that if we ever needed anything, their door was always open. I was shocked because they barely knew us!

Big Daddy dropped Li'l T off at school, and I was home alone, making sure I had everything packed and ready for when I went to the hospital. Baby girl was due in just two weeks, and I was overjoyed. I couldn't find my digital camera, so I figured it was still packed away in the basement in some boxes that we hadn't unpacked yet. On my way down, I must have missed a step because I tumbled down the five remaining steps. I tried to get up, but I couldn't move. I'd left my cell phone in our bedroom so I couldn't call Big Daddy, and I was too far away for the Google home box to hear me.

I noticed I was lying in a puddle of water. Where had the water come from? No one had been down here.

I shifted my position to get up, and that's when I noticed the water coming from between my legs. I gasped. I didn't know what to do because I was unable to lift my one leg and my water just broke.

I lay there and cried, *"Lord, I need you. Help me through this."* As soon as I said, *"Amen,"* a supernatural strength came upon me and I was able to use my arms to crawl to the top of the steps.

I opened the back door and crawled outside. My neighbors were outside tanning and when they saw me crawling, they rushed over and called 9-1-1. When the paramedics arrived, I was fully dilated so I had no choice but to deliver baby Bella right outside, on our patio. After four big pushes, baby Bella was out. My heart overflowed with joy just from looking at her and holding her in my arms. She was so beautiful to me, and I fell in love with her the moment I had her.

Baby's Arrival

I sat on the edge of the hospital bed, holding baby Bella and admiring her. Her beautiful hazelnut skin was soft as cotton. Baby Bella weighed six pounds and fourteen ounces, and she was nineteen inches long. She was a nice and healthy baby. After spending two days in the hospital, we were finally going home.

Big Daddy and I were packing up the baby's things when someone knocked on the door.

"Come in," I yelled, assuming it was the nurse with our discharge papers.

"Hey, young lady." Andy came through the doorway.

I looked at Big Daddy, and he looked at me.

"Can I help you with something?" Big Daddy asked as he went to pick up baby Bella from her crib.

"I came to see my granddaughter if that's OK," Andy said. "Keisha, I know I haven't been the best father to you, and I want to make it right. I'm sorry for everything that I've put you through in the past. I know I can't change any of it, but maybe you can give me another chance. I would like a chance to be a better grandfather to the baby, if you'd let me."

"How many chances have I already given you?" I waved my hand in the air. "How did you even know I was here?" I asked, thinking of all the people that knew my due date and trying to understand which one would tell Andy. Yes, of course it was—

"I talked to your grandmother, and she told me."

"Well, thanks for coming." I returned to the business of packing up our things. "We're getting ready to go home."

"Do you need help with anything?" Andy stuffed his hands into his front pockets and bounced on his feet.

"No, my husband is here, and we got it," I assured him.

"Do you mind if I hold the baby for just a little while?" Andy asked.

"Nah, my man, I don't think that's a good idea." Big Daddy cradled Bella close to his chest and assumed a protective stance.

"I understand." Andy put his head down.

"Look, we have to finish getting this stuff together so we can go home. Thanks for coming," I told Andy.

"OK, well let me know if you need anything."

"Thanks," I replied with a fake smile.

I watched Andy walk out the door and immediately burst into tears.

"You good, babe? Don't let that nigga get to you." Big Daddy stepped over, cradling the baby in one arm, and rubbed my shoulder.

"Yeah, I'm good. I just don't understand why he would show up here like nothing had ever happened." I took a deep breath. "When I saw him walk through the door, I figured Ms. Maryanne told him I was up here."

"Fuck him! Let's finish getting this stuff together and go home. Be careful with your leg, baby. I don't want you to be limping on both legs." Big Daddy chuckled.

"Shut up, babe." I laughed with him.

~ ~ ~

A month had passed since baby Bella was born. She was so perfect. She looked just like Big Daddy, only she had my nose and grey eyes—which we couldn't understand since we both had brown eyes. I loved her so much, and I could tell Big Daddy loved her just as much. Ms. Marrero and my mom would each take turns coming over to help with baby Bella.

On this day, baby Bella and I were home alone. Big Daddy was working, and Li'l T was at school. I received a phone call from

Aunt Gina telling me that Ms. Maryanne was in the hospital, and things didn't look good. I packed up baby Bella's things, and we headed to the hospital. We pulled up to the hospital. Some of the family stood outside the entrance.

"Hey, everybody." I walked up holding baby Bella in my arms. "How is she doing?"

"They moved her up to ICU because her tongue swelled up pretty bad. It was blocking her airway, so they put her on a ventilator," Uncle Seymore said.

"Oh, wow. I'm gonna go see her." I adjusted baby Bella in my arms.

When I stepped off the elevator, the first person I saw was Andy. He stood by the coffee machine, fixing a cup of coffee, and didn't seem to notice me. I walked right past him and went over to Gina, who gazed out the window, deep in thought.

"Hey." I rubbed her shoulder. "Are they letting visitors go back and see her?"

"Yes, you can go back there now." Gina's gaze dropped to Bella in my arms. "Aw, give me the baby while you go see Mama."

"OK, please don't let anyone else hold her until I come out." I carefully transferred my precious baby into Gina's arms.

"OK, I won't." She started bouncing softly and gazed lovingly at Bella, who still hadn't woken up from the car ride.

I walked into the room. Ms. Maryanne lay there lifeless, while a machine was breathing for her. Tears ran down my face, my heart aching to see my grandma like this. I remained with her for ten minutes. Before I left, I prayed over her. When I walked out into the waiting room, Ms. Maryanne's Pastor was there to encourage the family. I glanced over at Gina, who now sat by the window with baby Bella in her arms. She still hadn't woken up from her nap.

"Well, I'd better get going, but before I go see Maryanne, I would like to pray with you all first if you don't mind," the Pastor said. We all grabbed hands and stood in a circle. Gina sat silently holding Bella and bowed her head. "I would like to encourage all of you and let you know that I'm here if any of you need me. Don't hesitate to call me. Maryanne is one of the mothers of the church, and we all are praying for her. I also want to let you know that life is short. You never know what could happen in just one split second. So, if you have a falling out with your sister, brother, mother, or father, then you should fix it while you still can. Because if you put it off, just when you decide to fix it, it might be too late." The Pastor then went into prayer.

When the Pastor finished praying, I headed over to Gina so I could get baby Bella, but Andy intercepted my path. As I looked at him and before he spoke, I thought about what the Pastor had said, how if we had a falling out with a family member, we should make it right before it's too late.

"I hope you can find it in your heart to forgive me, young lady." Andy stood in front of me, tears rolling down his face. "You are my daughter, and I love you very much."

"OK." Tears ran down my face as well. At that moment, Andy and I hugged and cried in each other's arms. My heart no longer held hate for him. He was my father and if he wanted to make it right with me, then I wasn't gonna try to stop him. I wasn't deciding to completely trust him—trust had to be earned—but I was willing to slowly work on it.

Baby's First Birthday

I sat at the kitchen table, making princess centerpieces for baby Bella's birthday party. Baby Bella would be a one year old in just two days. Big Daddy and I were having a small get-together for her. Of course, my mom and Ms. Marrero had a lot to do with the planning. I was going over the guest list when I saw Andy's name.

Since the day at the hospital, Andy had been keeping touch with us. Ms. Maryanne was out of the hospital—*thank you, Lord*—and she was back to her normal self again. I knew everything happened for a reason, and often I thought that Ms. Maryanne went into the hospital so that we all would get closer together.

~ ~ ~

It was the day of baby Bella's first birthday party. We rented tables so that we could have everything outside and so no one would have to go into the house for anything, except to use the bathroom. We used the black baby princess theme for everything: princess tablecloths, napkins, cups, and of course princess cupcakes. We had hot dogs, sloppy joes, and pizza. The dessert table had a little of everything: cake, cupcakes, pretzels, candy, and even a chocolate fountain.

Everything was perfect! We had a good time with our family and friends. We played games, took pics, and shared lots of great memories together as a family. Even though it was baby Bella's birthday, I had a great time with all the family. Andy and I took our first picture together. I'd never noticed how much we looked alike before, but I was the female version of him. Once the party ended, everyone started to slowly leave. Andy stayed back and helped Big Daddy and me clean up. After that we watched movies together.

I loved the way Big Daddy treated baby Bella, and I couldn't have asked for a better father for her and Li'l T. Deep down, a part of me wanted Andy to treat me like that, and I still wanted to be his little girl. But there was also a part of me that wanted to say fuck Andy and to move on with my life without him. I let him know that this was the last chance that I would give him, and if he messed up or disrespected me ever again, we were done for good. He'd been doing a wonderful job checking on his grandkids and buying Li'l T school clothes or whatever else Li'l T wanted.

Andy might have not been a great father to me, but he was trying to be a good grandfather. I forgave Andy, but I would never forget all that he'd put me through. I chose to move on with my life and focus on the future, rather than dwell on the past, especially since I couldn't change it. I wanted nothing but the best for my kids, and I wanted them to be proud of the woman I was. I would teach them to have forgiveness in their hearts, because without that a person would be miserable in life.

Shardae is a freelance writer from Lorain, Ohio, where she was born and raised. She is the author of the drama, romance novel *Young Luv*, published in 2015. Growing up, she enjoyed reading romance novels and writing poems. A member of the International Writers Association. She lives in Northeast Ohio with her husband and children.

www.ingramcontent.com/pod-product-compliance
Lightning Source LLC
Chambersburg PA
CBHW021159110726
47900CB00002B/651